He stared at her with disturbing intensity

"You'd be amazed, Alex, at the ends I'll go to, to get what I want," Justin finally said quietly. "And I want you back."

"Why?" Alex kept her voice expressionless.

"Why wouldn't I?" He leaned forward and ran one finger down her bare arm, his eyes resting on her tanned body. "I've touched you," he whispered evocatively. "And I want to keep touching you."

"You never give up, do you?" Alex snapped. "...I've my own life now, and it doesn't include you!"

"Alex, don't push me," he warned.

"I wouldn't dare! Not the great Justin de Wilde, whose word is law," she said scornfully.

Furious, he stormed off, while Alex sat watching until tears blurred her vision. He'd never know how desperately she needed him....

Play Our Song Again

by

LYNSEY STEVENS

Harlequin Books

TORONTO • LONDON • LOS ANGELES • AMSTERDAM
SYDNEY • HAMBURG • PARIS • STOCKHOLM • ATHENS • TOKYO

Original hardcover edition published in 1981
by Mills & Boon Limited

ISBN 0-373-02488-6

Harlequin edition published July 1982

CHAPTER ONE

HE stood under the hot jets of the shower spray willing the sensations to banish some of the tiredness from his body. And he was tired, in mind and body. His neck and shoulder muscles ached and his eyes felt gritty and strained as he closed them tightly and rinsed the soap from his hair. He could almost enjoy the feel of the water on his naked body, tall, taut, well-built. There wasn't an ounce of spare flesh on his six foot frame, the rigours of his profession, perhaps not generally realised, requiring his body to be physically fit and his stamina excessive.

Eventually he switched off the water and dried himself on a huge blue bath sheet, rubbing his hair as though the vigorous action could clear his sluggish mind. His hand moved over his jaw and, sighing, he reached for his shaving kit. Tonight everything was such an effort.

He ran a comb over his still damp hair and his eyes rested on the reflection in the mirror. Square jaw, high cheekbones, a serious face, all planes and angles, the lips well shaped, with a tendency towards sensual full- ness until he drew them tight, as he seemed to do most of the time of late, in an expression of cynical detach- ment. His eyes were an unusual shade, a light blue-green, depending on the reflecting colours about him, but they stood out starkly against his tanned face and thick dark hair, now liberally touched with grey at the temples. Distinguished, Margot called it—he grimaced. All in all, not an overly handsome face but not without its attract- tion to the opposite sex. Most women found him attract-

ive, he knew. Irritatedly, he walked into the bedroom
and, dressed in casual grey slacks and a short-sleeved
white body shirt, he moved into the sitting room, striding immediately across to the small bar and fixing himself a drink, topping his Scotch up with dry ginger ale.

He took a mouthful and frowned down into the
amber liquid before moving across to the window,
drawing back the heavy curtains and gazing through
the plate glass at the blinking lights of Brisbane that lay
below his hotel on the Terrace. Any other time the after-
dark panorama would have soothed him, relaxed him,
but tonight he felt a disquiet, a dissatisfaction.

Had the city—the friendly sunny city, everyone called
it—had it changed that much in six years? There seemed
to be more high-rise buildings and he knew there were
more freeways; he'd noticed that during his drive from
the airport this morning. He finished his drink in one
gulp and flexed his shoulders again. The rehearsals had
taken more out of him than they should have, and he
wondered if the few days' break he had had before this
engagement had been a total waste of time.

Almost savagely he dragged the curtains closed,
shutting out the twinkling lights, and he knew an un-
characteristic urge to smash the empty glass clenched in
his hand and forced himself to relax.

It wasn't the few days break he had had, break from
the torrid pace at which he had been driving himself
lately. And it wasn't the rehearsals that had taken their
toll of him. A face swam before him, and his lips tightened so that he almost welcomed the tap on the door of
his suite.

With his dinner set before him he felt a little better.
Tackling the juicy steak and crisp salad gave his
thoughts more to work on, drew them away from the
memories that came crowding in on him. The meal was

more than adequate, but when he sat back and lit up a cigarette he realised he hadn't tasted a mouthful and his jaw tightened again, his eyes narrowing as he gazed absently at the smoking end of his cigarette.

Perhaps it had been a mistake to come back here, although six years was surely long enough. He had thought it had been, or else he would never have made the commitment to come. He wasn't indispensable; Chris Williams could have taken this engagement.

The face returned, in all its gamin beauty, with such vivid clarity that he closed his eyes in an effort to wipe it from his mind. But that was impossible, of course. It was a picture seared in his memory for all time. He could drown himself in his work, leave no time for reminiscences, but suddenly, after months even, it would reach back to clasp him. Some innocent catalyst would strike the right chord and flick him on the raw. It could be a sheaf of silky hair swinging down a street somewhere, a smile on a pixie face, a song she used to sing in her pretty, unremarkable voice. Today, it was this city.

God, why couldn't he simply put it behind him and forget her? Because for the first time in your cool ordered life you did something that wasn't planned, to which you gave no thought, he told himself. You did something on impulse, spontaneously, and it rebounded on you, crashed about you and shook your strictly conventional world.

He supposed, in some part, all that was true. He had led a formal and well planned existence. He preferred it that way; he always had. For as long as he could remember it had been that way for him. His family lived music, both parents being members of the Australian Symphony Orchestra, and he had cut his teeth on a violin bow. His mother had wanted him to excel on the violin, his father the piano, and although he had more than mastered both instruments he had followed his own aspirations and was now the much celebrated conductor of that very same orchestra.

Although his parents had now retired they followed his career with enjoyment and pride. In fact, he had spent his two days' break with them in their home, a sedate house with an adequate garden in the outer Sydney suburb of St Ives. They now taught music to keep up their interest, or perhaps to make up for what they considered their failure.

He stood up abruptly and crushed out his cigarette with an irritable movement. Even his parents were getting to him these days. He had lived with their disappointment over Ben for so long he was beginning to think along the same lines.

To his younger brother, music was simply something you switched on to help you relax, to dance to, to romance by. He smiled crookedly to himself. And Ben did plenty of romancing. Poor Ben! In his youth he was always in trouble for daydreaming, for missing music lessons. Now that he was a reasonably successful producer in an up-and-coming film company his torturous music lessons had been left far behind him and he knew Ben had made a good and satisfying life for himself in his chosen profession. Not that his parents had need to force *him* to follow them in his career. He had always known that music was part of him, just as Ben had known it wasn't the career for himself.

His brother's handsome face joined his pictures from the past and he saw them together, the dark piratical good looks, the fair hair tossed back as she laughed at something Ben said, probably outrageous. They laughed a lot together. They were more of an age, the same temperaments. Like feathers, soft and beautiful, drifting on a breeze lifting, soaring, floating, their touchdowns light and short before they rose again, as you reached out to clasp them, so easily crushed when caught.

He raked a hand through his hair. God, he was being fanciful tonight! Maybe he needed this holiday more than he realised. He knew he had been pushing himself, but he had been powerless to put a stop to it. Or perhaps the thought of this engagement had been slowly eating away at him and he had subconsciously over-compensated. He had known about their schedule. He had known about it for the past eight months, but he had been sure he could handle it.

Throwing himself into a comfortable chair, he passed his hand over his face. In all probability she wouldn't be living here any more and he was putting himself through all this for absolutely nothing. There was no certainty that she would come back here. She could be anywhere—Melbourne, Adelaide, Perth. Abroad. He stood up again and prowled about the room before walking exasperatedly across to his briefcase and taking out a folder of papers his accountant had prepared for him to look through.

His leather-covered address book was in his hands before he realised he'd lifted it out and his piercing eyes watched almost clinically while his long fingers turned the pages until a group of numbers almost sprang out at him. He looked down at the telephone and without thinking he lifted the receiver and dialled the desk. Why not try the number? She wouldn't be there, but at least he could say he'd made the effort. Why shouldn't he ring his wife while he was in town even if they had been separated for six years? The number rang hollowly in his ear. Surely they could be civilized enough to speak to each other. They . . .

'Hello.'

He didn't recognise the feminine voice.

'Good evening. May I speak to ... Miss Marshall, please?'

'Oh, I'm so sorry. We bought the house from the Marshalls four years ago. I believe they moved to Canada to live with their married son.'

'Oh!' He expelled the breath he hadn't realised he'd been holding.

'We have no forwarding address, so I've no idea how you'd contact them. I do hope it wasn't important.'

'No. No, it wasn't important. I'm sorry to have troubled you.'

He replaced the receiver. Canada. Well, that finished that. He turned back and picked up his papers, beginning to turn them over. Just three days of engagements and then a whole month's rest. After Saturday he could shake the dust of Brisbane from his shoes.

'Hey, Alex! How about we hit a night spot?' asked the young man at the wheel of the early model Ford station wagon heading through the now less congested city traffic, drawing to a halt as the intersection lights changed to red.

'Great idea, Paul,' came a voice from the back seat. 'We'll be in that, won't we, Jeff?'

'Sure will. What about Pipps?'

'The only night spot I'm going to hit is my comfortable bed. That's bed with a capital B.' Her voice was low and a little husky, and she flicked back a strand of silky hair that shone like shot silver in the dimness of the car.

'Oh, Alex, don't be a spoilsport,' said Paul persuasively.

'Yes, Alex, you could be missing the chance of a lifetime. Mr Right may be there tonight. Hey, sounds like a pop song.' He made a drumming beat on his knees.

'Trust you, Danny,' remarked Jeff.

'Mr Right at an ear-rupturing disco? You've got to be kidding, Danny!' replied Alex. 'Besides, I'm twenty-four years old and the only guys that I'd be likely to meet there might, and I emphasise the "might", have turned twenty-one if I'm very lucky. You can drop me home on the way and then you three can hit the high spots without me to cramp your style.'

'Some times you're the original dumb blonde, Alex,' said Paul. 'You'd be the best looking bird there. Even if you are a bit long in the tooth,' he added with a chuckle.

'On second thoughts you'd better not come along. We'd end up having to fight off the guys when we could be going for the girls,' laughed Danny. 'Oh, lovely young things they are, too.'

'Well, if you want to mix with giggling seventeen-year-olds, most of whom couldn't carry on a decent conversation if their lives depended on it, then who am I to pass comment?' she teased.

'Who needs conversation? We can get that from you, Ice Maiden.' A smile creased Paul Denman's narrow attractive face. 'You're behind the times, love. All talk and no action is definitely out.'

'Definitely way out,' agreed Jeff, his red head bobbing. 'You're too hard on the chicks, Alex. Weren't you ever seventeen and just a little foolish?' asked Paul.

The smile died on Alex's face, while Paul negotiated a sharp corner, unaware that his teasing words had found a chink in the fair girl's armour. She felt the pain, a knife's thrust, as the words found the old wound and set it aching.

'I guess I was,' she spoke with exaggerated lightness, 'some aeons ago.'

They laughed as Paul drew the station wagon to a

stop in front of a tidy old Queensland Colonial house
and Alex jumped out on to the footpath.

'We're all going along to the footie match tomorrow
afternoon if you want to come with us,' said Paul as
Danny took Alex's seat in the front.

'Oh, no, thanks, Paul. I . . . I have a few things to do
tomorrow.' Alex looked studiedly at her hand resting
on the car door ready to push it closed. 'I'll see you at
the usual time tomorrow night. Don't stay out till dawn,
now. You all need your beauty sleep.'

She walked up the wide front steps and inserted her
key in the right-hand door, turning to wave as the boys
drove way. The old house had been divided into two
spacious flats. Alex had one and the other was shared
by two schoolteachers. Alex liked to live alone, she
preferred her solitude these days.

Stepping inside, she closed the door behind her and
leant back against its solidness for a moment before
slowly crossing to her bedroom, unzipping the silky
sheath she wore and donning a soft terry towelling track
suit. She knew she should go to bed, but she was over-
stimulated, needed to wind down before she so much as
attempted to sleep.

Returning to the living room, she opened the side-
board and poured herself a small dry sherry. Perhaps its
mellow smoothness would help relax her tensed muscles,
her over-reaction to everything around her.

Of course, she knew exactly why she was tense, what
had set her on edge. And it was simply caused by a
chance of fate, a sheer coincidence. She crossed to her
old bureau, a memento from her father, and lifted its
roll top. The reason for her loss of equilibrium lay on
the desk, and she let her eyes move over it before lifting
the smallish sheet of paper.

At any other time she probably wouldn't have been

aware of the programme for the new cultural centre, but on that day two weeks ago the sheet of paper had lain in wait for her on the counter of a music store in the city. She had called to pick up a record that Danny had ordered and while the assistant had gone off to collect the LP, Alex's eyes had run absently over the record covers on display and then back to the counter.

The name in large letters had leapt off the sheet to hit her like a blow to the solar plexus. She had conditioned her mind over the years to reject all thoughts even slightly related to that period in her life, and to read that name while her defences were resting secure in the belief that he was interstate or touring abroad had shocked her into pale immobility. How she had completed the transaction of purchasing the record she simply couldn't recall, and it was only when she reached the sanctuary of her flat that she realised she also clutched the advertising bill along with her package.

In the two weeks since that day she had schooled herself not to feel shock at the sight of those printed letters. She could look at them now without so much as a flicker of her eyelashes, although the other coloured square of paper on the desk did send shivers of a kind of dreaded anticipation down her spine. She had forced herself to purchase that ticket, a ticket to the matinee performance tomorrow afternoon, and she would go along. For old times' sake, she told herself. After all, it was ages since she had treated herself to a little classical music. Real music, he had called it.

Once and for all she would prove to herself that he meant nothing to her any more, that the few brief months they had shared together were simply an encounter, a mere touching of her life upon his, a sparking of mutual desire, a searing flame that was doused the first time it was subjected to a dissenting breeze.

Their marriage had been a mistake. They were poles apart in every facet of their lives and a marriage between them could never have worked in a million years even if . . . She bit her lip, feeling the pain clutch at her again. She mustn't think about that. The years hadn't dulled that particular agony. Perhaps it never would.

Unable to stop herself, she reached into the bottom drawer of the bureau and lifted out an old photo album and laid it open. It was the only photo she had of him.

They made a perfect couple. She was so fair while he was dark, dark and ruggedly attractive. She looked dispassionately at her own laughing face. Had she ever been that young? She could hardly credit that she was now six years older. And was she six years wiser? She knew she had lost a lot of the youthful joie de vivre that shone from her eyes back then, the clear untroubled serenity she had before she had met him and her life had been thrown into a confusion of pleasure and pain.

And would the years have changed him? In the photograph his smile had softened the firm lines of his face, the seriousness of his usual expression, taking years off his age, and she felt a pang at his undeniable attraction. When he turned the charm of that smile on her she fell to pieces. At least she had in the beginning.

She sighed, running a finger over the surface of the photo. He would be almost thirty-six now, a gulf of a dozen years between them, years that they had thought would mean nothing compared with the pure attraction they had for each other.

In the beginning it had been good—she couldn't deny that. They had been physically attracted to each other— a purely chemical reaction, no more. If she had had any sense she would have simply gone to bed with him and got him out of her system. Plenty of her friends thought nothing of doing just that. She ran her fingers through

her hair and flexed her tired muscles. She could no more
have done that than fly. It had to be all or nothing. She
had wanted no hole-and-corner affair, and neither had
he.

And so they had married. And when the first strain
was put on their relationship it had folded like a house
of cards, a marriage she could have sworn would last
for ever. For ever. Nothing lasts for ever, she told herself
cynically. Nothing.

Well, all that was behind her. Six years' worth of being
alone was behind her, had been weathered, and she had
made a new life for herself. She had joined up with the
three boys as lead singer in their band and they had a
five-night-a-week permanent engagement in a popular
city restaurant. The four of them realised their luck in
this. It was more than anyone could expect in the business.

Tomorrow was to be their final night in Brisbane for
a whole month. The management wanted the band to
play down at their new restaurant at Surfer's Paradise on
the Gold Coast by way of building up its clientele down
there. They had even had their accommodation provided
in a large flat not far from the beach which belonged to
the owner of the restaurant. It was all just like a working
holiday for the four of them. They began next Tuesday
night and Alex had been looking forward to it.

So didn't that prove that she didn't need anyone or
anything? Especially him. Tomorrow afternoon she was
going to sit in the stalls and watch him, prove to herself
that it was definitely over once and for all.

She picked up the advertising sheet again, her eyes
skipping over the words, words she knew by heart.
Australian Symphony Orchestra. Limited engagement.
Featuring the internationally renowned soprano Margot
Donald and English tenor Graham Peters. And the

celebrated conductor Justin de Wilde.

Her lips twisted. So Margot was still in the play, waiting patiently in the wings. That was the one thing that she found hard to understand, that he had never sued for divorce and married Margot. Because Margot was biding her time for that moment. And she had everything on her side. She was the type of wife he should have chosen—nearer his age, poised, sophisticated, genuinely talented. Yes, Margot was more in keeping with his background, his career. Instead of an angry young folk singer with long fair hair, large blue eyes and a burning desire to change the world.

Next day Alex dressed carefully, in a subdued suit of pale blue, and wound her hair up into a chignon. She wanted to go unnoticed, to blend in with the crowd. On the offchance that he would cast a searching eye over his audience, she didn't want to call attention to herself.

As an afterthought she slipped her opera glasses into her bag as she ran outside and caught a bus into the city. At first she had planned to drive in, but it was simpler going by bus. She could relax and psyche herself up for the afternoon's performance.

That she needed to do just that was made clear to her this morning when she had innocently turned the pages of the *Courier Mail* and his face had leapt out of the paper at her. They had attended some function the evening before, after their performance, and the photographer had snapped them drinking champagne with the Lady Mayoress. Margot Donald's hand rested possessively on his arm and he had been caught leaning slightly towards the Lady Mayoress, listening intently to what she was saying.

The pulpy photo had not reproduced well, but it didn't detract from his distinguished attractiveness. She tried to decide how he had changed, for she thought he had in some almost imperceptible way. His hair looked to be whiter at the temples. Before it had only been peppered with grey. And the lines running from his nose past his mouth seemed to be etched a little deeper.

Now the members of the orchestra had taken their positions, were tuning up, while the audience chatted patiently. When he appeared there was a moment's silence before the theatre filled with applause. He acknowledged their welcome before striding into his position and calling the orchestra to attention.

Alex sat stiffly in her seat and almost cried out at the pain. It was as though her whole body had been numb and suddenly circulation returning brought the agony of renewed sensation. She remembered the way he held himself, tall, erect, the purposefulness of his stride, the way he inclined his head.

Oh God! It had been a mistake to come. She had to fight down an urge to rush from the theatre, but of course, she had left it too late. Far too late. Now his presence held her rigid in her seat, as though he exuded a magnetism that drew her to him, held her under his spell. It had been that way from the moment they'd met.

The concert auditorium faded away and she saw again the setting for that meeting, a chance encounter, that had such a disastrous effect on her whole life, her whole life style. She closed her eyes as the music swelled around her and that scene returned so vividly that the twanging music of the guitars and a banjo ringing in her memory almost drowned the swell of the Symphony Orchestra . . .

The Queensland sun shone brightly that afternoon, adding a shine to the pebble pathways across King George Square, reflecting off the symmetry of the City

Hall, giving the green lawn the appearance of a soft thick carpet. A rally was in progress and Alex was there with a few friends from the University. They were protesting peacefully about some injustice and there were speeches and songs and the distribution of pamphlets to passers-by.

The leader of the rally was an awesome sight—faded jeans, loose sweatshirt, thick dark hair and beard, tall rangy body. His bushy brows drew together as he thundered emphatically on his battered guitar. That he was one of the nicest, kindest, most peace-loving individuals that Alex had ever met seemed extremely hard to believe at that moment.

Someone in the crowd stepped forward to disagree with a statement and a heated debate broke out. The crowd sitting or lounging on the grass stood up, the better to observe the loud altercation. Alex herself had been sitting on the outskirts of the group, and standing on tiptoe, she took two or three hasty steps backwards in an effort to see over the bobbing heads in front of her only to career into a firm masculine body, which until that particular moment was striding purposefully across the square without a sideways glance at the intense little group.

In those split seconds before two firm hands came about her to steady them both she only had time to register the feel of a smooth silk shirt against her bare shoulder and the solid muscular body beneath its softness. As she turned to offer her apologies for her carelessness the words all but died on her lips. In fact she couldn't have said whether she actually voiced them or not as her startled blue eyes grew round as they met his eyes, cool and light in his tanned face, with just a flicker of something abstruse in their icy depths.

He was so ... No, handsome wasn't exactly the right

word to describe him. Yes, he was reasonably nice looking with a firm square face, straight nose and dark,
immaculately combed hair. But there was something else.
He was so ... perhaps compelling.

His hands slowly relaxed their grip on her arms and
he lifted one hand to smooth his unruffled hair. Alex
became aware of her own fingers still resting on the
satiny front of his shirt, feeling the steady thump of his
heart, and the intimacy of the sensation had her flushing
as she hastily dropped her hand.

'I didn't hurt you, did I?' she asked lamely, breathily.

A ghost of a smile touched the corners of his mouth.
'Only took me by surprise.' His voice was deep and
pleasant.

Those light-coloured eyes flicked over her hair, shining almost white in the afternoon sun, her face, lightly
tanned and freshly youthful, her slim body clad in the
tight old jeans and curve-revealing shirt, before returning impassively to meet her gaze. Alex's blush deepened,
much to her mortification. It was as though he had
actually reached out and physically touched her.

'I'd heard that Queensland girls were very friendly,
but I didn't expect one to throw herself into my arms!'

Straightening her back, Alex lifted her chin, only to
see the humour in his face that brought a certain boy-
ishness to his chiselled features, and she wondered fleetingly if he was perhaps younger than she had at first
thought.

'Just joking,' he said lightly, and this time he did
smile.

Alex actually felt her knees wobble. She had read
about such an occurrence in books, but she had always
disdainfully discounted such a feeling as romantic nonsense. But now she had the absurd urge to sit down
before she fell down.

'Are you part of these angry young people?' he asked
evenly, those seeking eyes skimming the crowd, not
giving any indication as to whether he admired or con-
demned such a gathering.

'Kind of,' she heard herself reply, and cringed inwardly. What in heaven's name was wrong with her,
acting like a gauche schoolgirl? 'Observing mostly.' She
forced her unwillingly dry lips to form the words. 'A
friend of mine asked me to write a report on the rally
for the Uni newspaper.'

He nodded. 'What seems to be the basis of the protest?'

He showed no inclination to move on, and suddenly
Alex found she wanted him to stay, so she launched
herself into an objective coverage of the whole thing, all
the while aware of the compelling aura about him, all
the while sensing that he was something more than just
an average passer-by. His silk shirt, tailored slacks and
conservatively expensive leather shoes put him into a
much higher wage bracket than herself and her family.
That he actually listened to and commented on what
she was telling him also warmed her to him. So much so
that when one of her friends hailed her she knew a spurt
of disappointment that he would continue on his way.

'Hey, Alex! We're all heading back. You coming?'
called a tossled-haired youth.

'Oh no. No, I'll stay on a little longer,' she replied,
hoping the stranger would too, as she turned back to
him.

'You have some interesting ideas, Alex,' he said, using
her name quite easily, and his eyes flicked over her again
before he added, 'Would you care to join a visitor to
your city for coffee and more conversation?'

Alex was taken aback. Her first thoughts were of the
pitfalls that a girl could encounter allowing herself to be

picked up by a stranger and she hesitated uncertainly, wanting desperately to see and know more of him but knowing she must follow the rules.

'No. I'm sorry, I don't think I should. Thank you very much anyway,' she said softly, feeling very young and unsophisticated.

'Because you don't want to or because we haven't been formally introduced?' he smiled back.

'Oh, no. I'd like to very much, but . . .' Alex blushed at her eagerness.

'Well, may I make the introductions? I assure you I'm a most respectable member of the community. I'm at present staying at the Gazebo up on the Terrace, and here,' he drew a brown leather wallet out of his pocket and showed her a folded piece of paper, 'is my driver's licence. Justin de Wilde from Sydney. How do you do, Miss Alex . . .?' He raised one dark eyebrow as he held out his hand.

In a reflex action Alex found her hand going out to him. 'Alex Marshall,' she said as his long fingers folded about her hand and a tingling sensation spread from that contact.

'Just Alex?' he queried.

She shook her head slightly. 'Alexandra.'

'Well, Alexandra Marshall? How about it? I passed a coffee shop a couple of doors up the street. We might be lucky enough to find a vacant seat.'

She wavered uncertainly as his hand stayed clasped around hers and those eyes rested on her face. 'All right,' she agreed at last, and he smiled as though he was genuinely pleased she had accepted. That had been the beginning. And the end.

The deafening applause penetrated Alex's thoughts and she almost started as she once again became aware of her surroundings. A tight band of tension enveloped her head and her fingers were stiff where she had clutched her hands together in her lap.

As Margot and the tenor reappeared to take another bow the applause rose again. Margot brought the two long-stemmed red roses with which she had been presented to her face, savouring their delicate perfume, before she blew three or four theatrical kisses to the audience. Of course, they loved it.

And Alex couldn't deny the fact that Margot Donald was a striking-looking woman, with her auburn hair, pale complexion and perfect figure. Besides her good looks she was an exceptionally talented soprano who spent as much time singing overseas as she spent in Australia, receiving rave reviews everywhere she appeared.

Stepping across to centre stage, Margot presented her conductor with one of her roses with exaggerated deference. As Alex watched all this something twisted inside her and she forced her eyes closed as Margot put her red-tipped fingers to her lips and much to the delight of the fans, blew Justin de Wilde a kiss. Curtsying again, Margot lifted her hand in a sweeping gesture of her acknowledgement of the conductor and he turned and bowed to the applauding crowd, a small smile lifting the corners of his mouth.

Alex's hand instinctively raised her opera glasses to his face, bringing it vividly closer, and she assimilated each feature. Those intense light-coloured eyes seemed to be looking straight at her and she froze. But his eyes turned away as the curtain fell.

Alex remained where she was as people around her began to file out of the rows of seats and out of the theatre. Her eyes gazed unseen upon the luxurious fall of red curtain, and she tried valiantly not to admit to herself that an old wound within her had begun to throb as she had watched the familiar exchange between Margot and Justin. And what had she accomplished by seeing him again? she asked herself. Absolutely nothing, she answered without a shred of truth.

CHAPTER TWO

ALONE in his dressing room Justin de Wilde shed his
immaculately cut jacket and lowered himself into the
one comfortable chair in the room. He closed his eyes
and sighed heavily. The tiredness was still weighing
depressingly upon him. He unbuttoned the cuffs of his
shirt and then the collar, running his hand tiredly
around the back of his neck, feeling the stiffness of his
taut muscles. One more performance.

After a while he reluctantly glanced at the time and
grimaced. He had less than an hour to shower and
change in readiness for the dinner Margot had arranged
they attend. Now he wished he had refused to go along
with the arrangements. It would be another wretched
farce.

God, he was sick of it all! All the glitter, all the pretence, the continuous maintaining of the façade. He
could feel his muscles tensing and ran a hand over his
eyes before forcing himself to relax back into the chair.

He could almost hear the ticking of his watch as time
raced on and he knew he should force himself to snap
out of it. Exasperatedly he moved decisively to his feet
and his hand caught a folded newspaper resting on the
small chest of drawers by his chair. Retrieving it, he
straightened the pages and glanced halfheartedly at the
local headlines. He had intended reading it before the
matinee performance, but somehow time had slipped
away from him again.

It was something of a habit he had fallen into in the
last few years, to buy at least one local newspaper in

each city he visited. Goodness knows, usually he was too tied up to see anything of the centres where the orchestra performed. So he tried to substitute this lack with a little local news.

As he turned the first few pages, his eyes skimmed the various articles—local and overseas news, the racing guide, the cartoon section. When he found himself half smiling at the Charlie Brown strip he shook his head and turned the page. Advertisements, entertainment—the whole double page was devoted to places to dine, to dance, movies.

Sighing again, he went to cast the paper aside when the photograph of a heart-shaped face framed by long fair hair almost sprang out of the page at him. He stared at the fuzzy print, scarcely believing his eyes.

It had to be her. He felt his muscles knot in the pit of his stomach and he sank once more into the chair as his eyes read the small advertisement. Christies' Restaurant. Dine and Dance to the music of the Everglades. For the first time he realised that hers was one of four faces in the small photograph. Three men and Alex. So she was still singing.

He reached over and lifted the telephone book from beside the phone and flipped the pages. Drawing a blank under de Wilde, he tried Marshall. Marshall, Miss A.M. and the address of a flat in Toowong. Why hadn't he thought of the phone book before? He had assumed she had gone to Canada with her parents, but she had been here in Brisbane all the time. His lips thinned as his eyes moved back to the photograph. Well, now that he had found her, what was he going to do about it?

'You're quiet tonight, love?' Paul Denman leant in the doorway as Alex finished fixing her make-up. 'Where's that sexy smile we all know and love?'

'I guess I'm just a little tired, Paul. I didn't sleep very well last night.' Alex gave her hair a final brush and turned a smile towards the lead guitarist. 'How's that?'

'Almost as bright as usual.' He touched a finger to the smoothness of her cheek. 'But it doesn't reach your eyes, Alex. Want to tell Uncle Paul all about it?'

'It's nothing, Paul. I'm really, simply tired.'

Paul sighed. 'Okay, love.' He smiled crookedly, his narrow face attractive in a melancholy way. 'I'm going to keep on trying, you know. And one day you're going to forget to hold me at arm's length.'

'Oh, Paul! You know I value our friendship, but . . .'

'But the chemistry's wrong?' he finished. 'We could give it time to react. You might enjoy it.' His dark eyes teased her. 'Sometimes slow burners explode into a very healthy old fire.'

Alex shook her head as she laughed reluctantly. 'Come on, we're due on stage in five minutes. It's a wonder Jeff hasn't come looking for us.'

'You're sidestepping me again, Ice Maiden,' he said softly as they walked down the narrow hallway. 'I wonder who the guy was who hurt you so much you won't let anyone halfway near you?'

Alex was glad they had reached the door to the small stage and there was no time for her to reply to Paul's question, had she been able to answer it. He was right, though, she knew that. She did keep everyone at arm's length. And on the couple of occasions that Paul had kissed her, light friendly kisses, it was as though her feelings, her senses, were frozen. Perhaps that part of her had ceased to function, had shrivelled up and died along with her marriage.

She tried to shrug off the wave of depression that washed over her. The fact that this was their last show at Christie's for a month didn't help at all, and she

stepped out on to the stage with a disquietening sensation that there was more than the poignancy of a last
show hanging over the evening.

The elevator soared smoothly upwards, travelling ex-
press to the top floor, and at eleven p.m. it contained
only one occupant. The doors slid silently open and the
man stepped out into the foyer of Christie's Restaurant.
The thick-pile red carpet and brushed velvet Regency
wallpaper served a dual purpose: not only did it give the
impression of opulence but it muted the sound of the
music and voices from within the restaurant.

The receptionist looked up from her desk before the
entrance to the dining room and her smile, which began
as a pasted on, part-of-her-job type of smile, quickly
turned into a genuine smile of interest as her eyes encountered the tall dark man striding across from the lift.

—'Good evening, sir,'

'Good evening. I phoned for a reservation. De Wilde.'
He smiled and the girl's eyes filled with admiration.

'Of course, Mr de Wilde. A table for one,' she reluctantly glanced down at the book in front of her, 'at the
back of the dining room.' She looked up at him, wondering at this particular request, but he refrained from
enlightening her and she was forced to motion to the
waiter who hovered nearby ready to direct the newcomer
to his table.

The restaurant itself was as richly decorated as the
foyer and judging by the number of patrons it was a
popular place. The subdued lighting served to screen his
entry into the dining section and he ordered a Scotch
and dry before consulting the menu.

However, immediately the waiter left with his order
his eyes turned to the spotlit stage in front of the small
dance floor, which was packed to its capacity with

gyrating couples. From this angle he was slightly side-
on to the stage and he watched as the music slowed and
the lights on the dance floor dimmed. She raised the
microphone she held and began singing. He couldn't
say he had heard the melody before, but she gave the
sadness of its lyrics an added pathos and his eyes
remained fixed on her for the entire song.

Lit by a spot, she was seated on a tall stool and the
velvet-like material of her rich dark wine-coloured catsuit shone in the highlight as she swayed slightly with
the beat. Justin's eyes moved over her hair. It was as
long and lustrous as he remembered and seemed to
appear almost white under the lights. Memories flooded
back over him, memories of its silken feel as he ran his
fingers through it, how it twined about them in tangled
disorder as they made love.

The familiar pain twisted deep within him and he cast
the menu on to the table, his lips set in self-derision. He
was acutely aware that his anger flared up against her,
because he couldn't deny that she still had the power to
stir him even after six years.

His eyes returned to her profile. He knew the long
dark lashes shielded blue eyes that could deepen to
indigo when . . . His lips tightened. Her nose was small
and straight with just a slight tendency to turn up at the
end, and he knew her lips were soft and pliant.

At that moment she turned slightly in his direction
and those same lips were moving, forming the words,
her face sad with the ballad of lost love she was singing.
The corner of his mouth rose cynically at the sentiment
behind the song.

From this distance he couldn't say that she had
changed very much at all. She certainly didn't appear to
look any older than she had looked when he had last
seen her and he couldn't repudiate the fact that she was

every bit as attractive as she had always been. His hands
clenched on the table top and the waiter had to address
him twice before he was even aware of the young man
standing beside his table. Because it was expected of
him he ordered a light supper he had no interest in eating
and then his eyes returned to the stage.

She was standing now, hands clapping to the up-tempo
beat, and the three young men were singing in harmony
with her. None of the three other members of the band
looked to be any older than their early twenties, and he
noticed that they were all quite good-looking. And their
music was faultless—he gave them that.

He recognised the song as one of Neil Diamond's
early numbers—she had always liked Neil Diamond's
recordings—and he watched her body swinging to the
beat. She was not a short girl and he supposed before
she had been a little on the thin side. Now he could see
she had added a little weight, her catsuit moulding her
nicely curved contours. She had gained weight in all the
right places, he thought wryly, and glanced around the
restaurant at some of the other diners.

Most of them were smilingly enjoying their meals and
the music, and his lips tightened as he noticed that more
than one pair of male eyes were turned to the stage and
gazed admiringly at the blonde-haired singer. Anger
flared within him as a fleshy man at the next table
remarked a trifle loudly to his friend on the attractiveness of the female entertainer. The two men laughed
together and Justin had to quell a desire to thrust his
fist into the man's face and throw him and his friend
bodily from the room.

He took a long swallow of his drink. This was utter
madness. What did he care after six years? For all he
knew she could have found consolation in any number
of men's arms. His eyes ran over her again. No, he didn't

want to believe that. But she was a free agent and the break-up of their marriage and subsequent separation cancelled any obligation she had to him. Nor had he any right to make any stipulation to her about how she lived her life.

He finished his drink and stared moodily into the empty glass. It had been pointless to come here tonight, absolutely pointless. What had he hoped to accomplish anyway? If he'd had one shred of sense he would have let it be, gone off tomorrow without a backward glance. But what was he doing? Sitting drinking, gazing at her like a frustrated youth.

As the waiter passed he ordered another Scotch, wishing he was capable of drinking himself into oblivion. How many had he had since the end of the performance? Three? Four at the most? Margot had all but accused him of being tipsy before he left. She had been livid when she announced his disinclination to attend the 'after the show' party she had arranged at her hotel. He could have gone along and enjoyed himself without putting himself through this fiasco. Then he would have been off to Hayman Island in the morning with little more than a slight hangover.

And if it came to that, exactly what did he expect to come of this evening? That they would be able to sit down and talk? Perhaps share a couple of drinks? All very civilised. And then go their separate ways. What could be simpler? He almost laughed out loud. Had he really deceived himself into believing it could be that way? Their parting had been washed with such bitterness, how could he even imagine that a few years' separation would wipe the slate clean?

He looked up frowningly. Where was the damn waiter with his drink? The waiter was nowhere to be seen, but another man approached his table and Justin looked at him blankly when he smiled a greeting.

'Mr de Wilde. Good evening. What a pleasure to have your company at Christie's.' There was just a trace of accent in the man's speech and his short stout appearance and thick waving dark hair suggested he was from south-eastern Europe. He wore an immaculate dark suit and a white dress shirt, and Justin rose a little reluctantly and took the hand that was held out to him. The handshake was firm and decisive, but Justin was in no mood for a doting fan.

'I'm Chris Georgi and I own this place,' the man smiled. 'It's not often we have such a celebrated patron. My wife and I attended your performance last night. Most enjoyable. We're both great admirers of your work.'

'Thank you.' Justin inclined his head and found himself smiling back at the man's genuine compliment, and he motioned to the empty chair. 'Won't you sit down?'

'Thank you.' Chris Georgi subsided into the empty place. 'May I buy you another drink?'

'I have ordered one.' Justin looked around as the waiter materialised beside him and the restaurant owner waved the young man away before Justin could sign for the drink. 'You have a nice place here.'

'Yes. It took a while for us to get on our feet, but in the past few years we haven't looked back. We're opening another restaurant next week, down at Surfers Paradise on the Gold Coast. I'll be happy if it's only half as successful as this one.'

The band started up again and both men turned towards the stage.

'They're not bad, are they?' remarked Chris Georgi. 'Just the kind of pleasant sound you need as background music while you dine.'

'Yes, they are good.' Justin's eyes moved again to the

girl as she began singing.

'That's Alex Marshall.' Chris's eyes followed Justin's.
'Looks great, sings great. And she's one of the nicest
girls I've met in this business. The band will be down at
Surfers for the opening on Tuesday and I'm keeping
them there for a month or so.' He smiled to himself as
he watched Justin's eyes remain intently on Alex.
'Would you like me to introduce you?' he asked
seriously enough, although his eyes danced teasingly.

'Oh, no, I don't think so.' Justin turned back to the
other man, a fixed smile on his face. 'I'm looking forward to my supper,' he changed the subject easily. 'Does
the food taste as good as it looks?' he asked as the two
men at the next table were served.

They chatted until Justin's order arrived and then
Chris Georgi excused himself and Justin was left to eat
his meal alone. At least he wouldn't have to pretend an
enjoyment he wasn't feeling. But surprisingly he found
he was hungry, and once he had eaten his head seemed
to clear and he felt a little more in command of himself.
Perhaps he had needed the food to banish the effects of
the alcohol.

He sat back listening to the music, enjoying a cigarette
with his coffee, and was surprised to note that the dining
room was now only half full. His wristwatch told him it
was drawing close to closing time. Through the cigarette
haze he exhaled, his eyes narrowed on his wife's figure.

A quarter of an hour later he stood up and after settling his bill he asked to see Chris Georgi and was directed
to an office door off to the right. Before he could change
his mind he strode across, rapped on the door and went
inside.

Those patrons remaining in the restaurant applauded
enthusiastically as the Everglades' final song drew to a

close and the four young people left the stage. Sighing tiredly, Alex went straight to her dressing-room and slowly began collecting her make-up together.

Resting her chin on her hands, she gazed at herself in the mirror. She could see the strain of the afternoon there in her face and underneath her make-up she knew the dark shadows lay beneath her eyes. Her jaw felt stiff with the effort of smiling and she gently massaged her temples, trying to dispel some of the aching tension. If only she'd stayed away from that wretched performance! It had been a mistake to see him again, to rake over old coals.

'Ready, Alex?' Jeff banged on her door. 'We've got most of the gear all set to go in the wagon.'

Alex pulled herself together and hastily collecting her bag and make-up case she joined Jeff in the hallway and they walked along to the now empty dining room. Most of the lights had been switched off and only those about the stage glowed brightly. Paul and Danny were lifting a large amplifier on to a trolley which they used to transfer their equipment downstairs to the station wagon.

'Grab the other end, Jeff,' Danny strained under the weight of the amplifier. 'You too, Alex. You know we're small lads and every little bit helps.'

Alex laughed. 'You don't need me, you're doing fine. Besides, I love watching all those muscles flexing,' she chuckled.

'What muscles?' Paul hunched his shoulders as they set the amplifier down. 'We're musicians, not weight-lifters.' He smiled. 'Looking forward to our few days' break?'

'Sure am,' she replied with feeling.

'Me, too,' added Jeff. 'I guess we may as well get the gear down to the car.'

'You sure you don't mind taking a taxi back to your flat, Alex?' frowned Paul. 'I could run you home first.'

'No, Paul, of course I don't mind. It's the most practical solution. The equipment plus the three of you in that poor station wagon will be stretching it to its limits as it is. I'll meet you down at the Coast some time tomorrow or early Monday.'

'Okay, I'll tell Chris we're leaving.' Paul moved to cross to the office. 'Oh, here he is now. We're off, Chris.'

They all turned towards their employer as he strode into the circle of light. Behind him moved another figure bathed in the muted shadows. The tall figure stepped from behind Chris's stocky frame and as the light fell on his face, Alex froze to the spot. She was totally incapable of speech or movement as she struggled to swallow in a mouth suddenly dry with the shock she had received.

'You've had a most celebrated audience tonight,' Chris was saying, 'and as he enjoyed your performance I thought you might like to meet him.' He turned to include Justin in their circle. 'Paul Denman, Jeff Martin, Danny Lane and, of course, last but by no means least, the very ravishing Alex Marshall. I'm sure you've all heard of Justin de Wilde.'

The lights caught the flash of silver hair at his temple as he shook hands with each of the young men in turn. Alex's eyes remained fixed on his profile, a profile she knew by heart, had not forgotten one single contour of, and she waited with racing pulses for him to turn to her.

'Miss Marshall.' His eyes met hers, steady, controlled, expressionless, and he held out his hand.

The contact between them burned like a flame in Alex's cheeks and she dragged her eyes from the web of his, fighting to portray an outward calm she was far from feeling within her. What could he be playing at? Obviously he wasn't going to acknowledge their association. Association? She felt the corner of her mouth twist cynically and knew those eyes wouldn't miss her fleeting expression. But she had to say something. She could see the frown of concern on Paul's face as he watched her cheeks flush and then pale.

'How do you do, Mr de Wilde.' She found her voice with difficulty and tried to control its waver.

'Wouldn't have expected you to go in for our type of music, Mr de Wilde,' grinned Danny. 'We're most flattered.'

'On the contrary, I enjoy all music, especially when it's well performed.' His tone was pleasant enough, but Alex noticed his smile didn't quite reach his eyes. 'You have a good sound.'

'Thanks,' smiled Danny. 'If you want to talk classical stuff then Paul here's your man. He's crazy about it, has stacks of classical records.'

Justin's gaze turned on Paul and the younger man shrugged his shoulders and grinned lopsidedly. 'Nobody's perfect,' he quipped.

'Quite.'

Justin's eyes left Paul to return to Alex and she felt that Paul was watching them both. Paul was altogether too perceptive, and the last thing she needed now was for him to begin asking probing questions.

'Ah, Alex—your taxi!' Chris struck his forehead with his hand. 'It completely slipped my mind. I'll go and ring you one right away.'

'I'll take Miss Marshall home.' Justin's deep voice halted the restaurauteur as he made to return to his office. 'That will save her having to wait for a taxi.'

'Oh, really, I couldn't put you to the trouble.' Alex's

heartbeats fell over themselves in agitation. 'I don't mind waiting at all, Chris,' she added almost desperately.

'It's no trouble,' Justin said evenly, his light eyes piercing into her mind, until she felt he was aware just how reluctant she was to be left alone with him.

'That's extremely kind of you, Justin,' Chris smiled innocently. 'There you go, Alex. A hire car is much more comfortable than a taxi.' He put a friendly hand on Justin's broad shoulder. 'You know, we don't trust Alex to just anyone,' he teased.

Alex flushed again and Paul's forehead puckered enquiringly.

'Well, the sooner we get this gear downstairs the sooner we can get home to bed as well. See you down the coast, Alex.' Danny moved over to the trolley and they all began to follow him.

All except Alex. She found it impossible to make a move, and Chris and Justin looked at her questioningly.

'Shall we go, Miss Marshall?' His hand went out to take her elbow and the pressure of those strong fingers willed her to start towards the door.

'Glad to have met you, Justin,' said Chris as he left them. 'See you next week, Alex.'

CHAPTER THREE

OF course it was impossible for them all, plus the equipment, to fit into the one elevator, so Alex found herself alone with Justin in the silent sterile confines of the purring lift. Paul's narrow features, set in lines of perplexity, stayed in her mind as the door slid closed.

She was certain Justin would be able to hear the thump of her heartbeats as they rose deafeningly in her ears to thunder almost painfully. Tilting her head forward, she fixed her eyes on a spot on the carpet at her feet and her hair fell about about her face, successfully shielding her expression from his probing gaze. And his eyes were on her; she didn't need to look at him to know that. She could feel their touch burn over her and she shivered slightly as the door glided open and she could stumble out of the confined space like a drowning man surging into an air lock.

She should run, just break away, leave him standing there. But as the thought was relayed from her brain those long sensitive fingers took her arm again and turned her firmly towards the exit to the car park. They still hadn't exchanged a word as he settled her into the passenger seat and closed the door with a subdued click that seemed to demand she remain where she was while he moved around to his side and slipped on to the bench seat beside her.

As he rested his arms lightly on the steering wheel, she sensed him turning and felt his eyes on her again. Like a moth drawn to a flame her eyes were compelled from her hands clutched together on her lap and she turned her head to meet the steadiness of his gaze.

Through the haze of pain that engulfed her at the familiarity of that face, the straight nose, firm chin, square jaw, she heard him sigh. 'Well, Alex, it's been a long time.'

Alex only trusted herself to nod her head. She must remain cool and calm, must not let him suspect that their years apart had made little or no change to the way she felt about him. His nearness still had the power to set her traitorous body pulsing for his touch. 'What made you come back, Justin?' she asked quietly.

He smiled humourlessly, feeling that same stirring of his senses at the low huskiness of her voice. 'I could say to see you,' he replied, and watched the colour flood her cheeks in the glow of the interior light. He looked away and his hand flicked on the ignition. 'It's the first engagement I've had in Brisbane in recent years. I thought I'd look you up.' His hands competently swung the car out of the narrow parking space and turned left on to the city street, taking the freeway exit to Coronation Drive.

'Things have changed around the city,' he remarked, and Alex dragged her eyes from his hands moving expertly on the wheel and looked unseeingly out over the dimly lit river.

'Yes. You must have a little trouble finding your way about with all the new one-way streets and freeways.'

'Actually I haven't had a lot of free time to get out and about. I rarely seem to these days. My engagements are usually fairly tight, so,' he shrugged, 'it's a case of all work.'

Silence fell between them, only broken by the low purr of the engine, and Justin turned the car away from the river and was soon moving slowly along Alex's street.

'You ... You know where I live?' she asked in surprise, realising she hadn't mentioned her address.

'From the phone book,' he said levelly. 'Which house?'

'The white one on the left.'

The car stopped smoothly and he switched off the ignition, moving out to open her door for her, taking her make-up case from her nerveless fingers.

Surely he didn't expect her to invite him inside? But he walked along the pathway beside her and waited quietly while she unlocked her door with a less than steady hand. Remaining on the top step, she reached inside and switched on the foyer light so that they were bathed in the glow through the open doorway. Facing him, she held out her hand for her case.

'Thank you for driving me home,' she said, hoping he would take the hint from her tone and leave, but she should have known better, of course.

Ignoring her hand, Justin stepped past her into the flat. 'It seemed a good opportunity to speak to you,' he said in that same even tone, looking about at the simple but pleasant decor of the living room, then slowly setting her case on to the floor.

'What ... What did you want to talk to me about?' She stood stiffly just inside the doorway, her mind moving in slow motion.

He gave a soft laugh and sank on to the lounge seat. 'Nothing in particular. Old times. New times. What's wrong with that? Surely we can be civilised?' He could almost laugh at himself. His feelings at the moment were far from civilised, if she but knew.

'Of course.' She tried to match his ease. 'It's just that I'm a little tired. I've ... I've had a long day and I still have some packing to do.'

'Ah, yes. You're going down to the Gold Coast. But you can spare me a few minutes?' His smile only lifted the corners of his mouth momentarily. 'After six years? Why don't you sit down and relax?'

Alex subsided into the farthest chair from his lounging figure, wishing this just a dream, a crazy nightmare, and that any moment she would awaken to find it was pure fantasy. What could he want anyway? she asked herself. They could have nothing to say to each other. Nothing. It had all been said six years ago.

A thought crossed her mind with painful suddenness. Divorce—it had to be that. Justin had come to ask her for a divorce. Her face paled as she felt the knife edge of that word sear through her.

'That's better,' he was saying, his eyes moving around the room again so that he missed her fleetingly stricken look. 'You have a nice place here. But then you always had a flair for decorating.' He glanced back at her.

Alex strove to pull herself together. 'Thank you. I . . . it's not a bad flat and very convenient,' she said, feeling trite. 'I took it on when Mum and Dad went to Canada a couple of years ago to help my brother and his wife with their new business over there.'

He nodded. Alex's parents had not been in favour of her marriage to him. It was all too sudden. She barely knew him. She was too young to know her own mind. And Alex knew Justin had felt their animosity towards him.

Justin watched her through half-closed eyes. She used to be quite a timid little thing, like a bird, and he would never have imagined she would be able to exist alone, stand so well on her own two feet. She appeared to be managing admirably and for some reason this thought did not sit easily on him.

'How about a cup of coffee?' he asked, and watched irritatedly as she stood up and hurried into the kitchen, her expression one of thankfulness to be getting away

from him. With lithe grace he stood up himself and went
to follow her out of the room, then changed his mind,
shoving his hands deep into his pockets and prowling
about the living-room.

Standing in front of the wall unit, he flipped through
a small pile of LPs and then ran his eye over the books
on the shelf above the stereo outfit. They were arranged
neatly, apart from one, which had been shoved hori-
zontally on top of the others. He lifted it down.
Elizabeth Barrett Browning's *Sonnets from the
Portuguese*. One corner of his mouth lifted. She had
always been a romantic, loved poetry. This was her
style.

He opened the book and the flourishing writing on
the title page caught his eye. 'Darling Alex, the Happiest
of Birthdays. You know how I love thee. Paul.' He read
those words twice before snapping the book shut and
throwing it on to the shelf. A cold white anger took
hold of him, twisted deep within him, and his hands
clenched futilely.

So she had been finding some solace all these years.
Somehow he really hadn't thought she would have. God,
he was naïve! Why shouldn't she feel the need of a relationship with a man? he sneered at himself. Why not,
indeed? From the first their own relationship had been
physically explosive and Alex had been as easily aroused
as he was, had matched his rising passion with her own.

He felt his muscles tense and swung irritably away
from the sight of that leather-bound tome. The room
was suddenly hot and he reached up to loosen his tie,
unbutton the collar of his shirt, and then shrugged his
arms out of his suit jacket, throwing it on to the lounge
chair where he had been sitting. He flexed his shoulder
muscles. That felt better.

His eye was caught by the sight of another jacket

draped over the arm of the third chair in the room and
he lifted it, holding it up. It was obviously not feminine
and his lips thinned as he looked about the room for
any more signs of masculine occupation, wondering
angrily why he hadn't thought of it before now. She
could be living with someone for all he knew. His anger
glowed brighter and, not stopping to think, he crossed
the lounge in long strides and swung open the bedroom
door.

The double bed covered by a colourful Indian weave
spread seemed to mock him and he swallowed the bitter
taste that rose in his mouth as his eyes flicked over the
room. The dressing table was all feminine and a half
full suitcase lay open on the bed. However, he could see
nothing to indicate that a man shared the room.

Alex returned to the living room carrying two mugs
of coffee, and at the sight of Justin closing her bedroom
door she paused on one foot, her face mirroring shocked
surprise. Slowly, she set the mugs on the low coffee table
before she turned back to him. And anger had replaced
her surprise.

'Just what do you think you were doing, Justin?'

Unconcerned, he sat back down in the lounge chair
and lifted one of the mugs of coffee. 'Looking about,'
he replied, sipping the dark liquid, his face showing no
sign of contrition.

'With what in mind exactly? Scouting out the area?'
She stood stiffly looking down at him, her face flushed
and her blue eyes angrily disdainful. 'Well, think again,
Justin! And on second thoughts, you may as well leave.
It's late and we have nothing to say to each other.'

He sighed, seemingly unmoved by her outburst,
making no move to do as she directed. 'Sit down, Alex.
I was simply ascertaining the fact that you were or were
not living here alone. I thought a little detective work

would be less painful than asking straight out.'

Her colour deepened at the implication behind his words. 'I'm living alone and I like living alone. So now that you've discovered what you came to find out perhaps you'll be kind enough to leave me to continue living happily alone!'

One corner of his mouth lifted almost bitterly. 'Alone seems to be the operative word. Are you sure you're not protesting too much, Alex?' He raised his hand as she drew a sharp breath. 'Calm down. What was I supposed to think? I saw that jacket on the chair and it crossed my mind that you might have been sharing the flat.'

'With a man, of course,' she stated sarcastically.

He shrugged his broad shoulders and her eyes moved involuntarily to the ripple of muscles beneath the fine material of his shirt. 'It was a man's jacket.'

'It belongs to a . . . a friend.' She paused almost imperceptibly before she used the word, angry with herself for offering any explanations.

'The thin dark-haired young man I met tonight?' It was more of a statement than a question.

'The three of them are good friends,' she said flatly.

'What have you been doing these past years?'

The abruptness of the change of subject had her blinking for a moment before she answered. 'Working,' she replied carefully. 'I've been with the Everglades for four years, two of those years at Christie's.'

There was a moment of silence and she watched him as his eyes appeared to be fixed on the coffee mug he had clasped in his long sensitive fingers.

'What about yourself?'

He looked up then. 'Working, too.'

'You've obviously done well.' Alex swallowed a lump that inexplicably threatened to rise in her throat. 'I . . . I suppose your parents are very pleased.'

A slight frown washed over his face. 'Yes, I suppose they are,' he replied in a tone as flat as her own.

'Are . . . are they enjoying their retirement?'

'I think so. Dad has the time now to spend in his garden.' His frown deepened. 'He hasn't been very well these past months, has to take things a little easier.'

Alex was genuinely perturbed. 'I'm sorry to hear that. What's the trouble?'

'His heart. He had a mild attack just after Christmas, although he seems to be out of danger now. But you know how my mother fusses over him.'

Yes, Alex could imagine. Justin's mother was an extremely forceful woman and although Alex knew she did care for her husband and sons Grace de Wilde always gave the impression that she ruled her family with an iron hand. When Justin had first taken her to meet his parents his mother had terrified her, giving her the distinct feeling that she was found wanting as an adequate wife for the elder de Wilde son.

His father had been totally the opposite. He had taken Alex as a daughter, and the fact that he would have been upset when he learned that she and Justin had separated had caused Alex some disquietening feelings of guilt in the early days. And she felt a twinge of that same guilt now, wishing she could personally wish him an improvement in his health.

'Ben's up here in Queensland filming something or other,' Justin was saying.

'Yes, I know.' Alex smiled crookedly at his look of surprise at her words. 'He . . . he called to see me a couple of months ago on his way up north. He's doing a documentary on the Great Barrier Reef for the National Conservation people and then I think he said he was beginning on some kind of adventure-cum-thriller set in the same area.'

Justin was watching her through half-closed lids, his jaw set tightly. 'I didn't realise you two kept in touch,' he remarked a little sharply.

It was Alex's turn to shrug her shoulders. 'He usually phones or calls in when he's in Queensland,' she said simply.

'I see.' His tone added volumes to those two words, and Alex's hackles rose.

'No, I don't think you do see, Justin,' she said quietly.

His head rose and it crossed his mind that she was even more self-possessed then he had given her credit for earlier, and he had to admit that the knowledge threw him somewhat. She used to be so . . . so . . . biddable. Added to this revelation was the familiar stab of—envy? Jealousy? call it what you like, that always assailed him before when he witnessed the rapport Alex seemed to have with Ben. She had no trouble relaxing with his brother, laughing, and teasing him as much as he teased her. At times Justin had almost wanted to lash out at his brother, and if Ben had been here at this moment, he would have done just that.

With dire difficulty he pulled his thoughts into order. 'You don't think so? Well, just what is it I don't see?' The low controlled quality of his voice had an ominousness that was not lost on Alex.

'That Ben and I are friends.'

'Friends. Oh, just friends,' he repeated.

'Yes, just good friends. Sometimes you're lucky enough to meet people you click with,' she tried to explain, 'and you just feel a kind of bond with them. Even if you don't see them for years when you do meet up with them again you simply pick up where you left off. There's nothing male-female about it. You're simply friends.'

His lip curled sardonically and Alex shook her head a little exasperatedly.

'I can't see any reason why our conflicts have to make any difference to my friendship with Ben. Why should it? For heaven's sake, Justin, if he had to take sides he'd have backed you without hesitation. He all but worships you,' she said shortly, her anger rising because she should feel she had to justify her actions.

This new Alex was becoming more of a surprise to him, and rather than putting him off, he found it was only adding to the attraction she had for him. Justin put his empty coffee mug on the table and stood up moodily, thrusting his hands into the pockets of his slacks. 'I never suggested that anyone should take sides,' he said, his back to her.

Alex found her eyes taking in the dark hair lying over his collar, the width of his shoulders, the narrow waist and tapered hips, and she knew a sharp pang of regret that she was not still able to run her hands over the firm smoothness of the body beneath. She had always had such pleasure simply touching him.

When she made no comment he turned around, surveying her through brooding eyes. 'There shouldn't have been anything to take sides about.' His voice had dropped lower, his words causing Alex's heartbeats to accelerate wildly.

Her breath came sharply through her cold lips and momentarily she wished what he said was true, that nothing had come between them, that she could feel the joy of going spontaneously into his arms. But too much had happened, to drive a wedge that forced them apart until the gap had widened and finally severed the tie.

A feeling of panic rose within her, panic that the conversation was getting out of hand, would touch on a subject she had no desire to rake over tonight or any night, and her reply came out harshly in her distress, sounding biting to her ears. 'Well, there was, and fortunately it's all water under the bridge now, so there's simply no point in talking about it.'

'What you mean is, sweep it under the rug and pretend it's not there.' His tone matched hers. 'Just as we did from the moment we were married. Everything got swept under the rug until we had a pile so high we couldn't see our way over it.'

'Justin . . .' she began, but he cut in on her.

'Well, it's the truth. We were at cross purposes right from the start. The only time we ever agreed was in bed.' His eyes raked her flushed face. 'When we had to move back to Sydney you wanted to be in Brisbane. When we moved into my flat you wanted a neat little house with a garden. Oh, not forgetting the nine-to-five husband.'

And children. The words screamed inside her head and a pain twisted deep inside her, opening the old wounds with callous ease and seemingly cold-blooded simplicity. To want children—was that wrong? Her fingers turned white where she convulsively clutched the arms of her chair as, pale-faced, she watched him stride across to lean menacingly over her.

'Well, Alex? Isn't that the truth? You didn't want a husband, you wanted a robot you could manipulate.'

She gathered her faltering control. 'Get out, Justin! I don't have to listen to this. It's all old news.' He gave a short mirthless laugh. 'We said it all six years ago and nothing's changed.' Alex tried to meet his gaze without flinching. 'We're still not treading the same path.'

'I don't recall us trying to discover an alternative road, one we could both follow,' he said clippedly. 'You wouldn't even consider attempting to discuss it, to talk out our differences like civilised adults.' He straightened up, running a hand through his dark hair, his eyes still on her face, focusing now on the agitated tremble of her full lips. 'But then we never took much time to talk, did we?' he said softly, suggestively.

Her eyes met his and she read that same expression in their light depths that she had years before. It was a very thin film covering the flame burning there and she caught her breath helplessly. Once she used to live for that sign of wanting and she was aware of the answering need in herself. If Justin had touched her in that moment she would not have denied him.

Dragging her gaze from his, she fought to remain indifferent to him. Nothing had changed. Here they were trying to talk, but to talk was the last thing they both wanted. An hysterical laugh bubbled inside her. Actions spoke louder than words, didn't they?

'We've been through all this before,' she repeated slowly and distinctly, clutching at what little control she had left, thrusting it between them like a barrier.

'And when we did talk it was at each other, not to each other. It's not the same thing,' he said flatly, his eyes still fixed on her.

'One thing's the same, Justin. It all had to be your way,' she retorted bitterly, 'and that's how you want it now.'

'Ah, yes, I'm the wrongdoer and you're the wronged. I'm always the one who just doesn't understand.' His voice was quiet with cold anger. 'You never missed the chance to accuse me of not caring about your precious feelings. Well, I did care, more than you knew. More than you wanted to know.'

'Justin . . .'

'Don't you think I suffered seeing you lying there in that hospital bed, so ill and . . .' he cut her off, leaning over her chair again. 'Oh, believe me, Alex, I suffered. I suffered knowing I was the one responsible for it, knowing I put you there, that I was the one who got you pregnant.' He swung away to the other side of the room, as though he didn't trust himself to be near her. 'I flaming well suffered,' he said with feeling.

'I didn't say you didn't. But you never wanted our child, Justin, you can't deny that,' she said quietly, getting stiffly to her feet, facing him across the living-room where he stood, feet apart, hands thrust angrily into his pockets.

'No, I'm not denying it. But you hardly gave me time to get used to the idea.' He rubbed his jaw tiredly with one hand. 'Look, Alex. I wanted a family eventually, but I needed to have you to myself for a while before we had a child.' He watched her face set coldly and made an exclamation of exasperation. 'Face it, Alex. Ninety per cent of men would have felt the way I did. Even that admirer of yours in your group, the one with the sorrowful spaniel eyes who moons over you so obviously. He'd feel the same way in the same situation,' he said cruelly.

'Then maybe I should try the situation on him,' she heard herself saying, insinuatively, 'if only to prove to you that you're wrong on that score.'

Justin's eyes narrowed and his chin rose, and Alex felt the rekindling of her fear. 'Oh, let's leave Paul out of this. He's a very nice person and a good friend and doesn't deserve to be brought into this kind of discussion.'

He had taken a couple of strides across the floor and was now standing barely a foot away from her, his anger reaching out to touch her, bridging the space with its intensity, and she could feel the throb of the pulse at the base of her throat.

'He's a very nice person and a good friend,' he mimicked, his lip curling. 'Wooing you with books of love poetry.'

Alex glanced across at her bookshelves and her mouth tightened. 'More prying, Justin? You have been busy!'

'It's written all over him that he'd like to be more than friends with you,' he continued as though she hadn't spoken. 'If he isn't already!' he added cruelly, his eyes lashing her coldly.

'Paul is a good friend, Justin. And you're still judging everyone by yourself,' Alex was stung to retort.

'Oh, I am, am I? Well then, it won't matter if I react true to form. I'd hate to disappoint a lady.'

His hands snaked out and pulled her against the hard length of his body.

CHAPTER FOUR

HIS lips took possession of hers in a fierce assault, forcing back her head until she thought her spine would snap. Never before had Justin treated her so callously, and her fingers pushed ineffectually against the solid wall of his chest. Tears flooded her eyes and she moaned a soft protest.

The sound apparently penetrated the surge of angry frustration that drove him and he relaxed a little of the pressure his fingers were exerting on her arms, although he didn't let her go. His lips ceased their insensitive punishing and began a gentler, more potent demanding, his hands sliding around her, luxuriating in the softness of her body moulded in the velour catsuit. His fingers now sensuously probed her backbone, following it down until his hands settled on her hips, compelling her impossibly closer to the complementary contours of himself.

Alex knew she was drowning. She was being pulled under to whirl in the vortex of the mutual desire that flared and raged between them. Justin's lips moved to tease her earlobe, sending shivers of sensual feeling through her entire body. His hand moved upwards to her hair, twining its silvery softness about his fingers. Alex's own fingers clutched at his shirt front, slipping beneath his now open shirt, touching the remembered smoothness of his chest with its mat of fine dark hair, feeling the tempestuous thudding of his heart.

She knew she should push him away before she became incapable of doing so, and as his lips slid down her jawline to seek her lips again she turned her face away and held herself as far apart from him as his enveloping arms would allow.

'Justin, please! Don't . . .' she gasped, as his lips continued their competent caressing of the smooth creaminess of her neck.

'You don't mean that,' he said with conviction, his voice thick with his own awakened passion. 'I feel it here.' He put his lips to the racing pulse at the base of her throat.

Alex struggled futilely. 'Justin! This won't solve a thing,' she said huskily, swallowing the moan of pleasure his lips were drawing from within her.

'I think it will. In fact, I know it will.' He caught hold of the zipper in the front of her catsuit and drew it downwards, his hand moving over the silky smooth skin of her midriff. 'It will solve six years of wanting, of needing, of dreaming about this moment,' he said thickly, 'and you've been dreaming about it, too. I can see it in your eyes. You want it as much as I do.' His chin lifted arrogantly.

'No!' She tried to remove his hand, draw her catsuit together, but he simply held her firmly with one arm clasped around her while his other hand moved upwards to cover the fullness of one lace-covered breast.

'No,' she said again, her fight to subdue the surge of arousal making her voice low and ragged, and she tried to shake her head as his lips descended again.

'Yes.' His kiss demanded her response and Alex was no match for his mastery. She felt herself responding, could do nothing to halt that response as he expertly overcame her last meagre defences. Time became nothing and Alex simply allowed him to carry her along on the tide of their mutual need.

Raising his head, he kissed her chin, her nose, her eyelids, the expression in his eyes one of drugged arousal. Alex's mind had ceased fighting, had given in to the dictates of her heart and body. Her hands moved feverishly over the dampened bareness of his shoulders and back. Somehow Justin had shed his shirt and it lay in a crumpled heap on the floor. That he was as physically aroused as she was Alex was left in no doubt and he crushed her to him in almost desperation.

Lifting her effortlessly into his arms, he carried her through to the bedroom, setting her down on the softness of the large bed. Her suitcase and clothes were swept to the floor and his hard body followed hers and they clung together in feverish abandon. There was one moment when Alex's mind would have reasserted itself, but that moment passed as her traitorous body surged to match him in his sensuous demands.

It seemed to Alex that she had been slumbering emotionally for the past six years and it only needed his touch to unleash the engulfing tide that swept over her, leaving her spent and lifeless, hanging in a comfortable and cosy limbo from which she had no desire to surface, was just a little fearful of breaking out of. If she allowed herself to think rationally again then she would have to make excuses for herself, explain to herself why Justin had this power over her.

Somehow it was easier to seek the blissful oblivion of sleep, and if she was aware that a firm arm held her tightly to the relaxed hardness of his body then she put that from her mind as well. Would it hurt anyone if she simply enjoyed the closeness, the oneness, for just that little bit longer? No, it could hurt no one but herself.

The morning sun was just about peeping over the rooftop of the house across the street when Alex began to struggle through the filmy curtain of sleep. She stretched languorously and then was still. Her body was pinned to the bed at the waist and her arm encountered a warm body close beside her, his soft even breath playing over her bare shoulder.

Total recall came with screaming suddenness and close on its heels was abject horror at her own weakness. A shudder passed over her and she pressed her eyes tightly closed, knowing the shame of loss of her self-respect. Dear God, she thought, make it all a dream, a nightmare. Let me open my eyes to the normality of just another day.

But the weight of Justin's arm heavily relaxed in sleep was far too tangible to belong to any flight of fancy. Her eyes darted helplessly about the room, searching for some means of escape, but to do that she would have to move his encircling arm, and surely he would awaken. Just what she planned to do if she did get out without waking him she didn't know, perhaps dress quickly and drive away. If only she had finished her packing then she could have been away to the Coast.

She reached out with a tentative hand and slowly began to lift his tanned arm, releasing it immediately when he moved agitatedly. He muttered in his sleep, his arm tightening about her convulsively.

Alex's eyes flew to his face, taking in the untidy thickness of his dark hair falling over his forehead, the dark curve of his lashes on his cheeks, the soft sensualness of his lips now relaxed, taking years off his age, giving him an almost boyish attractiveness. A lump gathered in her throat and she swallowed painfully. If only they had made a success of their marriage, been able to overcome their differences. Her eyes moved over his face again. And their child, their son—would he have looked just like Justin, with dark hair and a firm chin and those incredible light blue eyes?

As she watched, her body pain-filled, his dark lashes fluttered and she was looking straight into his eyes, crystal clear and as burningly bright as the sunkissed blue water over white sand. His return to consciousness was faster than Alex's had been and his lashes fell almost immediately to shield the look in those eyes as his face seemed to settle in an expressionless mask. But just for mere seconds before his lips curved in an easy smile and touched the bare shoulder by his chin.

Alex's heart leapt as his caress caused an involuntary response and she flinched away from him with self-disgust.

The slight flicker of blue eyes was the only sign he gave of noticing her reaction. 'You're looking very delectable this morning, Mrs de Wilde,' he said softly, his arm still confining her to his side. 'You have the distinctive look of a woman who's been made love to, and very satisfactorily at that.' His eyes moved over her tangled fair hair and slightly swollen lips down to the swell of rounded breasts just above his encircling arm.

Alex closed her eyes as she felt herself colour and tried to pull away from him. 'You're disgusting,' she said huskily, hating herself as much as him.

Justin raised one dark brow, his smile lopsidedly cynical. 'Disgusting? Oh, I see.' His own voice was ominously low. 'That wasn't what you said last night. Last night you were . . .'

'I don't want to talk about last night, Justin,' she broke in, her hands moving agitatedly, pushing against the rock-hardness of him. 'Please let me get up.'

He moved slightly so that his leg now imprisoned her and his hand was thus free to glide lightly over the smoothness of her flat stomach to encircle one firm breast.

'You're too tense, Alex,' he said mockingly, 'and that's bad for your health and wellbeing—all the shrinks say so. You should relax.' His lips teased one tautening nipple. 'And I know the most enjoyable way to complete relaxation.'

Alex felt the stirrings of capitulation flood to the surface. 'No, Justin, let me go. I don't want you to touch me again.' Her voice rose sharply. 'Just get out! I never want to see you again. You revolt me!'

His eyes locked with hers once more, a grey coldness replacing the burning warmth of arousal. 'For God's sake, Alex, grow up! You weren't in any damn hurry to fend me off last night,' he bit out harshly. 'What's with you anyway? Still trying for your pound of flesh? Or perhaps you're still hankering after that robot you can switch on and off when the mood takes you?'

'I didn't ask you to come back. And I didn't want you to touch me.' Alex tried again to push his hands away.

'Like hell you didn't,' he growled. 'Then how exactly would you describe all that reciprocated passion you displayed last night? Play-acting? I think not. At least be honest with yourself. You wanted me to make love to you just as much as I wanted to make love to you. Deny that if you can?' His eyes flashed angrily.

Alex drew her breath sharply, shameful recollections flashing before her eyes like staccato stills on a movie screen, and she cringed inwardly. He was right, of course. It was the truth. She had wanted him—desperately.

And with this thought came the fear that he would discover that she had never ceased to love him, not for a moment, during the six years of their separation. If he even suspected, then he would expect to pick up her life where he had left off, and she couldn't allow that. They could begin again, and it would end again. They would come together perfectly in the intimacy of their mutual desire and then become strangers, antagonists in the cold light of day. She wasn't strong enough to take any more of that particular pain, any more uncertainty. The decision was hers right now.

'I . . . I was tired last night. I . . .' She took a steadying breath, putting as much conviction as she could muster into her voice. 'I don't deny I was physically aroused,' she heard herself saying so matter-of-factly, 'and I've never repudiated that you were—you are an attractive man. And, of course, you always knew how to arouse me. You're really quite an expert lover, Justin. But then I'm sure you've been told that before on numerous occasions.'

She almost lost courage to continue as his jaw tensed, his nostrils appearing to flare, and her heart leapt into her mouth. 'We've been apart six years. That's a long time. And as I said, I was tired. Perhaps any reasonably attractive man would have done. Or maybe I wanted to see whether you'd lost any of the—er—expertise I remembered.'

It took all of Alex's remaining self-control to meet his gaze without flinching. She could scarcely believe such things could have come out of her mouth, and her eyes were the first to fall.

Justin's expletive was not pretty, and his hands tightened their hold painfully. 'Well, have I?' he bit out coldly, his face pale.

'Have you what?'

He moved his head angrily. 'Lost any of my,' he paused, his lip curling, 'expertise?' he snarled.

Alex shrugged, trying to keep an outward appearance of nonchalance. 'Obviously not, wouldn't you say?' she said lightly.

His eyes spoke volumes, shooting sparks, and his fingers were biting into the flesh of her arm. 'Perhaps you ought to try for seconds. Just to give you an all-over average. It could be almost a second opinion.' He drew her forcefully against him, his lips crushing hers, mercilessly.

And half of her admitted she deserved it while the other half fought against him with all her strength. Any fight she could put up wasn't enough. In strength he could overpower her fivefold.

Then suddenly he had released her, thrusting her back against the pillow. He levered himself off the bed, striding unselfconsciously across the floor to retrieve his discarded trousers. His solid nakedness held a primitive beauty, and Alex watched almost mesmerised as his muscles rippled as he moved. She lay back where he had thrown her, one hand pressed to her swollen lips.

'Sorry to disappoint, Alex,' he turned as he zipped his brown slacks, 'but it seems I've lost a little of my touch. I must be getting old.' His eyes raked her from head to foot as she lay on the bed. 'However, quite frankly, at the moment you just turn me off.'

She heard him move about in the living-room as he collected his shirt and jacket, and then the front door of her flat closed with a decisive and very final click. By the time she reached the open window of her bedroom he had negotiated a swift three-point turn and the hire car was speeding away down the street.

Alex moved slowly back to the bed, sinking down on to the rumpled sheets, knowing without a doubt that it was unlikely that she would ever see him again. He would never return after the things she had said to him.

Had she really voiced all those hateful words? Had it all been necessary? Somehow she doubted it. After all, she could not honestly lay the blame for last night entirely on him. Their lovemaking had been a mutual thing, a coming together of two people who had hungered for each other.

She buried her face in her hands and when the tears finally came she sank back on to the pillows where she and Justin had lain together and cried brokenheartedly for the first time in years. The tears had been building up inside her and although she wept because she had lost him she knew that another part of herself had been lost as well. The young and vivacious teenager, with a heart full of idealistic love for a knight in shining armour, seemed at this moment to belong to another time, almost another century.

She had had the chance to try to make their marriage whole again and she had now severed the tie for ever. Oh, no, Justin would never come back, after all she'd said to him. She felt sure he would now sue for divorce and, once he was free of her, Margot would be waiting with open arms to make him the right kind of wife for a man in his position.

It was useless trying to tell herself that he had not mentioned a reconciliation with her, that he had taken what was available, what he was still legally entitled to take, because those thoughts in no way cancelled out the revulsion she felt for herself.

At least this break decided the issue. It was over and done with in one quick sharp incision. If she had allowed him to think she had forgotten all that went before then she would have been back six years, living on the edge of a precipice waiting for the break to come. He wanted a wife who went along with him, agreed with his ideas, and she could never have allowed him to swallow her personality and have retained her self-respect. She had done the right and sensible thing, she told herself. But for all that the sobs shook her body and she suffered the pain of her loss once again.

The trauma of the past hours had taken its toll and she drifted into an uneasy sleep. The shrill insistance of the telephone in the living-room woke her an hour later and she stumbled dizzily to lift the receiver, in that unguarded moment hoping it would be Justin.

'Alex? Hi there!'

Her heart plummeted depressingly. 'Hello, Paul.' She tried to infuse some welcome into her voice, feeling guilty for that first instant of disappointment that his wasn't the voice she had hoped to hear. 'You're an early bird.'

'I didn't wake you, did I?' He sounded contrite.

'No, not really. I was just dozing.'

'Good. We've finished loading up the gear and we're heading off now. When do you think you'll be leaving?'

'I'm not sure exactly, Paul. I ... I have to finish packing.'

'Well, we'll leave the key of the flat down at the Restaurant. We decided we'd at least unload the equipment today and then spend the afternoon on the beach. Want to join us?'

'I'm ... I'm not sure, Paul. I'll try. Which beach? Surfers?'

'Yep! I'd better go. Try and make it, won't you, you look divine in a bikini.'

Alex looked down and realised for the first time that she wasn't wearing a stitch of clothing, and she folded her arm about herself protectively.

Paul was chuckling. 'Well, see you down there. Oh, Alex, by the way, did de Wilde get you home all right?'

'Of course, Paul.' Alex's lips moved stiffly.

'Good. He—er—he seemed to be a human sort of guy, considering his position, I mean. He's quite a bigwig in his field, you know. What did you talk about on the way home?'

'Talk about? Nothing earth-shattering. We didn't really talk much at all.' Alex relaxed the vicelike grip she had on the receiver.

'You didn't mind having him take you home, did you?

For a moment there I had a feeling you didn't—well, you weren't too fussed about him.'

'Of course I didn't mind. Why should I?' Alex closed her eyes tightly. 'I . . . I must go and finish packing. I'll see you down there later. Thanks for ringing, Paul.'

'Yes, well, see you, Alex.'

The turquoise blue sheen of the water flashed almost painfully in the fierce mid-afternoon sunshine and, in fact, if one intended to gaze towards the swimming pool for any length of time sunglasses were a must. About the pool tall palms and bushy greenery provided a welcome shade, a tropical coolness, and quite a number of the guests were taking advantage of the low comfortable patio chairs set about under the trees and nearer to the water.

Justin de Wilde was stretched out on one of these chairs beneath a gaily striped fringed umbrella. A long cool drink, looking quietly potent, sat untouched on the nearby table, diamondlike beads of moisture gathering on the outside of the glass, developing a pool at the base. The ice cubes had long since melted away, but for all that it looked cool and refreshing.

Earlier in the afternoon he had spent some time in the pool, but his brief swim shorts, his only attire, had now dried and he was beginning to feel the heat of the afternoon again. In the few days he had been at the island resort his tan had deepened; he had the right type of skin to tan easily without burning; and more than one pair of female eyes had followed him as he swam a number of lengths of the pool with long seemingly effortless strokes, the sun glistening on the rippling muscles of his shoulders and back as he cut rhythmically through the water.

Now a pair of dark glasses shielded his eyes from the glare and he held an open book, one of the latest bestsellers, resting on his crossed bare legs. A gold medallion glittered on a chain around his neck and to all outward appearances he was totally engrossed in the novel. This fact, however, was belied as he rarely turned a page.

Justin sighed and let his eyes move around the pool and its vicinity. Fortunately the dark glasses disguised the fact that his book was not holding his attention, as he was aware that the two women sharing the table a short distance from him were simply waiting for an excuse to approach him. This knowledge, that they thought him interesting, brought him no pleasure. They were themselves quite attractive women, but he found their obviousness an irritation.

But then everything irritated him. Making polite conversation with everyone irritated him. Being pressed into taking advantage of the resort's facilities irritated him. Margot and Graham irritated him. He felt his mouth twist cynically. He damn well irritated himself.

He ran a hand through his hair which had dried a little stiffly from his swim in the pool and noticing the drink by his side he raised it to his lips and took a sip. He grimaced. The chill had gone off it, but he supposed it was still thirst-quenching. He set it back on the table and tried for the umpteenth time to pick up the thread of his story.

He had really been looking forward to this break, his first real holiday in years, and now here he was wasting it. He'd sat about the hotel for the past three days boring himself stiff.

At least today Margot had accompanied Graham on a boat trip out to the reef. Since he had joined them here on Sunday evening Margot had tried unsuccessfully to coax him out of his black mood. Little did she know that nothing and no one could have done that, with the exception of Alex, perhaps.

When he drove away from her flat on Sunday morning he knew he could quite literally have throttled her with his bare hands. Never before had he come so close to wanting to physically harm another human being as much as he had wanted to punish Alex that morning. And if he admitted it he was just as angry with himself for that night. Things had not gone according to plan.

Somehow he knew before he went that going to the restaurant was a mistake, but he'd gone anyway, to see her, maybe talk to her. That was all he had in mind.

What an expert piece of self-delusion that was, he thought wryly, when all the while he had had a vague idea that there was a chance they might find something of the feeling they had once had for each other. Some naïve fool he was!

He had decided to play it by ear, take it slowly, see if the memories of Alex that had haunted him could be put into some perspective if he saw her again. And he thought he had succeeded. Until he noticed how that young pup was looking at her with adoring eyes. That had hit him right where it hurt, and his blood had started to boil. Alex was still his wife, after all, and until he said the word she would stay his wife.

Of course, had he listened to his head instead of his damned bruised ego he would have let it rest there. But no, he had to stick his toes in, take her home, make a point of going into her flat with her. He knew she didn't want him to, but that had made him all the more determined. Wasn't he a rational, thinking, civilised adult? He laughed self-derisively. Oh, he'd been civilised all right.

'Darling Alex, You know how I love thee.' The words written in the book were branded on his mind and he knew he had lost control of himself and the situation round about him. He tried to convince himself that it was only that same bruised ego reacting, but he had a gut feeling it ran far deeper than that.

A picture of Alex in Paul Denman's arms swam before him and he put a hand to his jaw as it clenched tightly, the peaceful surroundings of the pool fading into a hazy insignificant shadow in that moment. That another man could kiss her, caress her, the way he had done was an agony he couldn't contain. She was in his blood, and he felt a light film of persperation bead on his brow at the anger he felt against himself.

His recollections of the hours spent with her only fanned that self-derisive flame. He had always prided himself on his self-control and while he couldn't deny that his body had delighted in her touch, the recipro-cated passion, he was now filled with revulsion at his lack of restraint.

No wonder she had been so scathing! And yet hard on the heels of that thought came the balancing memory of her own response. He would never believe that Alex hadn't been as aroused as he was. It had been as though the years between had never passed, and they were still in the first blissful months of their marriage.

He felt the familiar stirring in his blood and his whole body tensed. If he had started out to lay any ghosts he had failed miserably. Alex was there, a part of him, and her parting words made him shift sharply in his chair. Yes, he'd really blown the whole situation. When he was with her he acted completely out of character. So much for the controlled, the suave, the sophisticated Justin de Wilde!

'Justin darling! There you are!' Margot Donald swept across the pebbled paving of the poolside with all the grace and impact that surrounded her on the stage. In a bright emerald green sunsuit, her auburn hair neatly confined by a matching scarf, she appeared to be oblivi-ous of the attention she was attracting.

Justin felt himself cringe. At the moment he needed this aloneness, and he knew he could never hope to make Margot understand that need. She thrived only when she was encircled by people. He watched a small frown of annoyance cross her face at his lack of enthusiasm for her presence, although he had to admit she was a striking-looking woman. They had known each other from their student days, had even indulged in a brief affair that was halted when Margot left to expand her studies overseas. Justin had missed her for a while, but not lastingly. Not the way he missed . . .

When his mother touched delicately and, she thought, subtly, upon the subject of his remarriage, she usually just happened to mention Margot. And looking at Margot now he knew why his mother thought she would make him an ideal wife. She was attractive, poised, talented, but . . . If he was honest with himself he could see no farther than a heart-shaped gamin face and long silky fair hair, and no matter how much they dissented it would always be that way for him.

So what was he to do about it? he asked himself as Margot sank elegantly on to the low chair she had pulled rather disgruntledly to his side. If he had one iota of sense he would simply cut his losses, leave Alex to the boy with the sorrowful eyes, take up his life from here, and forget her. However, he didn't hold much for his acting sensibly where Alex was concerned if last weekend was anything to go by.

He tried to concentrate on Margot's ecstatic descriptions of the reef and he felt the now familiar grip of irritation rising within him. When the hotel paged him he had to stop himself from sprinting away to take the telephone call.

CHAPTER FIVE

'YOU know, you kids are great. If we get many more compliments I can see I'll have to give you a raise in salary.' Chris Georgi slapped Paul on the back and then blew Alex a very expressive kiss. 'Did I tell you we're completely booked out for tonight and tomorrow night?'

'Great!' grinned Danny. 'You don't suppose there's a chance that there'll be a scout from some record company in the audience, do you? One who'll make us all famous?'

'Listen to him! You mean you'd leave me in the lurch?' Chris appealed to the others. 'That's gratitude for you!'

'You know we wouldn't do that, Chris,' laughed Paul. 'We'd give you a couple of hours to get a replacement.'

Chris shook his head in mock reproach. 'How's the flat? Have you settled in all right?'

'Sure have. And we've made a fantastic discovery.' Paul put his arm around Alex's shoulders. 'Not only is she beautiful, not only can she sing like an angel, but she's a Cordon Bleu cook!'

'Hardly Cordon Bleu, Paul,' Alex smiled, knowing that her smile was merely a lifting of the corners of her mouth. 'I hide the empty cans in the kitchen tidy.'

'Well, we're none of us complaining, sweetie,' laughed Jeff.

Paul left his arm lightly around Alex's shoulders as they moved off to change for the evening's performance and, instead of walking on to the other dressing room with Danny and Jeff, he followed Alex into hers and closed her door. Knowing what was coming, Alex crossed to her small dressing table and picked up her make-up, steeling herself in readiness.

'Alex, are you sure you aren't sick or something?' asked Paul, all concern.

'Sick? How could I be sick living down here?' she replied quickly. 'All this healthy sunshine and invigorating body surfing—I've got a great tan already.' And she knew she had. Each day the four of them spent some time on the beach, sunbathing and swimming or riding their surfboards.

Paul looked at her levelly. 'I know, I know. All that's true. But the dark circles under your eyes are getting worse.' He gently moved his finger in semi-circles over her cheeks. 'I also know you're not sleeping. I can hear you moving about the flat when you should be getting your beauty sleep. What's up, Alex? You've been like this since we came down to the coast.'

Her eyes fell from his. 'There's nothing wrong, Paul. I think I've simply let myself get a bit run down. Maybe I need some vitamins.' She put everything she could into making her smile normal.

A frown still puckered Paul's brow and he sighed. 'Well, if you say so, Alex. I worry about you, though. You know how it is.' He smiled crookedly.

'There's no need to worry about me, Paul,' Alex put her hand on his arm. 'I'm fine—really. And you're truly the nicest, kindest person I know, and if I had any sense I'd . . .' She stopped, wishing it could be that easy. If only she could put everything behind her, start afresh. And she would go a long way before she met anyone as considerate as Paul. But . . .

'Snap me up?' finished Paul, smiling sadly. 'I wish you would.' He ran a hand up her bare arm and pulled her gently against him, his lips meeting hers, cool and tentative.

It was a pleasant enough, if unexciting kiss. Paul's kisses were like himself—gentle, without force, almost a needing for reassurance. And Alex allowed him to kiss her for much the same reason. She needed reassurance herself, needed desperately to be held, needed someone to care.

She closed her eyes and returned his kiss with a mixture of relief and compassion, because he was there when she needed someone. However, he took her response for encouragement and his kiss deepened, became a passionate demand, taking her completely by surprise. He pulled her closer, and suddenly it wasn't Paul's arms around her; the arms were strong and tanned; the lips weren't Paul's lips, they were full and sensual; his . . .

Alex felt herself freeze and pushed against him, a wave of self-revulsion covering her entire body. How could she have done it to Paul? she asked herself, watching him with wide and fearful eyes. His face was pale and he was breathing quickly, his hands still holding her arms.

'Paul, please—I don't . . .'

He felt her shudder. 'God, Alex, don't do this to me! Do you know how it feels, to be led on and then dropped cold?' He couldn't hide the hurt in his eyes.

'I'm sorry, Paul. I . . .' She ran a shaky hand over her eyes. 'I didn't mean to hurt you, believe me, but I . . . I . . .' Tears spilled on to her cheeks.

'Oh, Alex, don't cry!' Paul's face changed from hurt to concern. 'I shouldn't have come on so strongly. I'm an insensitive oaf.'

Alex shook her head. 'No. No, you're not. Nothing could be further from the truth. It's me. I . . . oh, Paul!' She went into his arms and sobbed on to his shoulder for a few moments before she regained her control.

Paul patted her sympathetically until she stood away from him and fumbled for a tissue to dry her eyes. 'You must think I'm such a fool!'

'No. But I know there's something troubling you and if you don't get it out of your system you really will make yourself ill. Can't you tell me, Alex? It may help to talk it out.'

'I . . . I wish I could. But I just can't.'

They looked at each other, but before Paul could comment there was a knock on the door.

'Alex? Paul? Five minutes to go, you two,' came Jeff's voice.

Paul sighed. 'We'd better get ready.' He hesitated a moment and then leant across and kissed her lightly on the cheek before going out of the dressing-room. As he was about to close the door behind him he hesitated. 'Alex, has it got anything to do with that guy you met on the beach yesterday?'

'On the beach? No, of course not. He's . . . just a friend from years ago,' she said quickly, and with one last level look at her Paul left.

Alex turned back to the mirror and began deftly to fix her make-up.

So Paul had seen her talking to Ben on the beach. No one was more surprised then Alex had been when he appeared out of the blue. As she walked slowly up the sand, squeezing the salty water from her hair, he had been striding down towards the surf and, for the first time since she had met him, she had not been pleased to see him. He was too close to Justin, at this time, and although Ben scarcely resembled his brother, as he stood talking to her there was a fleeting expression, an occasional mannerism that cut through her like a knife.

But that wasn't Ben's fault, and she took pains to

hide the anguish she felt and bubbled over about the group's success at the restaurant with a brittle exuberance. Ben didn't seem to notice. In his field everyone raved on.

He was filming on location on the Gold Coast and he had taken a unit for the duration of the particular sequence of his movie and expected to be in the area for a month or so. They had laughed together when he offered her a part in the movie.

Usually when Ben visited or phoned her they refrained from mentioning Justin, but on the beach Ben had broken that unspoken rule by telling her casually that Justin was holidaying on the Barrier Reef. However, after taking one look at her pale face he had changed the subject. He would be bringing a party from the film company to Christie's for dinner tomorrow night, and now she wished she had been honest with Paul. But what could she have said? Oh, what a tangled web we weave. She pulled a face at herself in the mirror.

Christie's Restaurant at Surfers Paradise was twice the size of its Brisbane counterpart and tonight, as it had been on the previous night, the entire place was filled to its capacity. Chris was right—it was a roaring success.

From her position on the slightly raised stage, a much more elaborate affair than the Everglades were accustomed to, Alex scanned the sea of faces for Ben de Wilde, but she was unable to pick him out. Admittedly the restaurant was subtly lit with subdued lighting while the stage was a blaze of spotlights, so she did have difficulty discerning features past the dance floor and the first few rows of tables. He would be there somewhere.

Their bracket drew to a close and they moved to the back of the stage for a break. The three young men walked across to the bar for a drink while Alex sorted through some books of sheet music for a particular song they had been requested to play. The dance floor was empty and the hum of conversation was accompanied by the clink of cutlery, and Alex was unaware of the approaching footsteps until Ben's voice claimed her attention.

'Hey, Alex! How about giving us your autograph?'

She turned to greet him, a smile lighting her face. Ben was standing by the stage all right, looking very theatrical in a rich maroon velvet suit teamed with a pastel pink dress shirt, ruffled at the front beneath his dark red bow tie.

But it was the taller man standing slightly behind him that caused the dimpling smile to fade from Alex's face. Cool blue eyes met hers expressionlessly and what almost passed for a polite smile touched his mouth.

'Hello, Alex.'

Even as she felt herself go cold with shock she was struck again by the difference between the brothers. Justin was several inches taller and a little broader than Ben and although he didn't have Ben's almost 'chocolate box' good looks, Justin's firm square jaw and high cheekbones gave him a rugged handsomeness. His unusual piercing light blue eyes added a compelling commanding quality.

'How are you, Justin?' She was amazed that her voice came out so calmly, so steadily.

'Can't complain.' His smile was cynical while his eyes seemed to move over her as though he couldn't stop the need to take in every contour of her body clad in a revealing strapless midnight blue evening dress that clung in the right places and swirled about her legs as she moved.

'You sounded great, Alex,' Ben said quickly, and Alex could feel he was a little wary of the situation. 'Better than ever, don't you think, Justin?'

'Yes,' Justin replied slowly, looking around the stage at their equipment. 'Whoever set up your sound system knew what he was doing.'

As complimentary as ever, thought Alex bitingly. 'Actually, Paul Denman's our sound man.' She looked straight at Justin. 'He's a craftsman where sound equipment's concerned. What he doesn't know just isn't worth knowing. I think he's exceptionally talented.'

Justin's expression never altered and Alex thought her barbs had missed their mark until she noticed the involuntary beat of a nerve in his tensed jaw and knew a surge of success.

'Which one's this oh, so talented Paul?' asked Ben, unaware of the band of tension about his brother.

'The good-looking dark-haired one,' replied Alex, warming to the fray. 'He's a favourite with all the girls.'

'Oh.' Ben raised his dark eyebrow and shot a sideways glance at his brother. 'Lucky girls!' he remarked exaggeratedly. 'How about joining us for a drink?'

Alex glanced across and was relieved to see Paul, Danny and Jeff walking back towards the stage. 'I'm sorry, Ben, we're due to start up again now.'

'Well, when's your next break?' Ben persisted.

'About half an hour, but really I . . .'

'No excuses. I'll come over and get you. See you later.'

Justin didn't say anything. He looked across in Paul's direction before turning to follow Ben back to their table, his back as straight and uncompromising as his expression had been.

Before she could begin to wonder why Justin was here instead of being somewhere up north where he was supposed to be the other three had rejoined her.

'Who were they?' asked Jeff. 'A couple of ardent fans?'

'No.' Alex had to make a decision and decided she had better tell as much of the truth as possible. 'Actually it was Justin de Wilde and his brother.' She turned back to the sheet music she had been scanning to hide the colour that rose in her cheeks.

'That guy from the Symphony Orchestra we met up in Brisbane the other night? What did he want?' asked Danny. 'Hey!' He grinned teasingly at her. 'Don't tell me, let me guess. You've made a conquest, Alex?'

'Don't be silly, Danny,' Alex snapped back.

'I do believe the girl is blushing, Dan,' Jeff joined in. 'That's a sure sign she's interested at the very least.'

'I am not interested in Justin de Wilde,' Alex raised her voice as Jeff flicked a switch on the amplifier. Although she wasn't standing close to the microphone the way the heads of the diners rose and the slight titter of amusement made it obvious that her words had been audible to part of the room, and Alex cringed with horror, her eyes squeezed closed. 'Oh, Jeff, how could you?'

Jeff had the grace to look contrite. 'Gee, sorry, Alex. I never thought about the mike,' he whispered. 'Maybe he didn't hear you anyway,' he added hopefully.

Alex gave him a withering look, her face still aflame. Justin would have heard her all right!

'I hope you don't secretly fancy him, Alex,' remarked Danny, ' 'cause if you do and he heard what you said— wow! I think you've blown it. He's going to be mad as hell. No guy wants to hear a neat-looking bird making that kind of public announcement, that's for sure. Does absolutely zilch for a bloke's ego.'

'Well, it's too late now,' said Paul gently, giving Alex a sympathetic look. 'We'd better get cracking and give everyone something else to think about.' Obviously he hadn't recognised Ben.

As their next break approached Alex grew more apprehensive. Surely Ben wouldn't want her to join them now, after what she'd said. Apart from Justin's anger Ben would have every right to be upset with her as well. He thought the world of his brother. She finished her song with a feeling of inevitability, and the boys set down their instruments.

'Come and have a drink, Alex,' invited Paul. 'You look like you need one.'

'No, thanks. I might go back to my dressing-room for a while. I've got a slight headache.'

'Oh, no, you don't, Alex,' Paul interrupted her. 'I'm not going to let you slink away into your shell. It was an unfortunate accident. Besides, Jeff's right, he probably didn't hear it.' He took her arm and propelled her down from the stage and headed her towards the bar before she could voice her disinclination to accompany him.

'Paul, I . . .'

'No arguments, love.' He nodded at the barman. 'One beer and a stiff Scotch and dry.'

'Paul, I hate Scotch, you know that,' she appealed to him.

'An orange drink as well,' said a deep authoritative voice behind her, and Alex swung around to find Justin standing far too close to her. 'I'll swap you the orange for the Scotch,' he said evenly.

His cold eyes rested on Alex's pale face and she swallowed nervously. It crossed her mind that he was like an impassive tensed snake poised ready to strike, and there was no doubt about who was to be his victim.

'Good to see you again, Mr de Wilde. How are you?' Paul held out his hand and smiled pleasantly.

Justin's hand was slow to shake the younger man's

and his eyes barely flicked over him. 'Fine, thank you, Denman.'

The barman set their drinks on the counter and Justin paid him for the three. He handed Alex the orange drink and picked up the Scotch. 'Will you excuse Alex?' he said, taking her arm firmly, and without waiting for Paul's reply he led her across to the dining section, leaving Paul standing staring after them.

His hand held her beside him as they walked and she could feel the body warmth emanating from him as her arm brushed the jacket of his lightweight suit. 'Justin, I really don't feel up to making polite conversation at the moment.'

'Polite? Are you sure you know what the word means, Alex?' His voice came out with ominous lowness and she knew his outward calm only thinly masked his smouldering anger.

'Look, Justin, I'm sorry" She raised her hands expressively. 'What else can I say? I didn't know that Jeff would choose that particular moment to connect the microphone. What you heard was completely out of the context of our whole conversation.'

'Save it, Alex.' His fingers were almost biting into her arm. 'Let's just say that I'm not going to have you discussing me with your friends, or whatever,' he said quietly as they reached Ben's table.

In her agitated state Alex at first thought that the table held a dozen people, but besides Justin and Ben there were only four others. It was simply that they were so flamboyantly dressed and all appeared to be talking at once. However, when Ben noticed their presence he called the table to some order.

'Hi, Alex! Come and meet everyone. The stars of our movie, Bindi Oliver and Tony Jason, and this is my co-producer, Mike Bramley, and his wife Meg. Everyone, meet,' he shot a quick glance at Justin, 'Alex Marshall, the songbird.'

All but thrusting her into the chair Ben drew forward, Justin sat down beside her, next to Bindi Oliver whose eyes strayed immediately to his set face. The seating capacity of their dining table had passed its limit and Alex found herself crushed up against Justin so that he had to turn a little to the side, his arm resting along the back of her chair. She sat as straight as she could, holding herself away from him, but there was no way she could keep his thigh from touching hers. She could feel the warmth through the material of his slacks and her dress, and her stomach churned as her senses registered their heightened awareness of him.

'You have a lovely voice, Alex,' Tony Jason leant across to smile at her, and Alex knew that that particular smile would have had a lot of this up-and-coming young star's fans swooning.

She managed to smile back and thank him for his compliment while Justin's leg seemed to exert an added pressure and she clasped her hands together in her lap, her colour rising.

'Knock off the charm, Tony. You've overwhelmed the girl,' laughed Mike Bramley.

'Not Alex,' laughed Ben. 'The only person I've seen overwhelm her is my mother.'

Alex couldn't bear to look at Justin, or Ben for that matter, and her eyes met Bindi Oliver's in time to catch the speculative look she was giving the three of them.

'So you're a friend of the de Wilde family, Alex?' she asked with honey in her voice, her long fingernails scarlet against the white cigarette she raised to her matching scarlet lips.

Alex couldn't find her own voice to reply as Justin chose that moment to move his leg against hers.

'We've known Alex for years,' Ben put in quickly, and turned to address Mike Bramley. 'Shall we put our proposition to her now?'

'Good a time as any,' he replied, and smiled at Alex. 'We've arranged with Chris to film a sequence in the restaurant and we'd like to have you and the boys doing the background music.' He looked critically at Alex's shocked face. 'You've got good bone structure and you should be very photogenic. I'd say you'll come over exceptionally well.'

Alex was stunned.

'You make quite an impression on the leading man,' smiled Tony Jason, 'in the script and,' he paused, giving her another of his charmingly limpid looks, 'in real life.'

Alex was fully aware of the tension that radiated from Justin and her peripheral vision told her he was keeping a tight rein on himself. However, the fact that his eyes were aiming daggers at Tony Jason didn't seem to be bothering the young man over-much.

What right had Justin to be annoyed anyway? she asked herself and smiled defiantly at Tony. 'I'm flattered, Mr Jason,' she quipped, 'when I think of the number of women who'd give their right arms to be sitting here with the famous Tony Jason.'

'Make it Tony, Alex,' he laughed, showing perfect white teeth. 'And almost famous,' he added, looking much more human, and Alex warmed to him. Underneath the façade of the star he was most probably a very nice person.

At that moment the band started up and Alex realised she should have been back on stage. As she went to excuse herself Justin's arm came around her waist in a firm hold.

'Now we can have that dance you promised me, Alex,'

he spoke for the first time since they'd sat down. 'Excuse us.'

He stood up with her, his grip tightening, propelling her towards the dance floor without giving her time to say a word.

'Justin, I can't dance with you,' she protested angrily, annoyed that he should act so overbearingly, 'I have to be up on stage.'

'They won't miss you for one dance bracket,' he said, drawing her forcefully into his arms and clasping her rigidly against his hard body.

Paul saw them at that moment and after his initial look of surprise he continued to follow their progress with unsmiling eyes.

'Justin, please . . .'

'Please?' Justin mocked, his eyes fixed somewhere over her head. 'So polite now, aren't you, Alex? Just consider yourself lucky that I'm only dancing with you. The way I feel right now, if we were alone I'd probably strangle you.'

Casting a quick glance at his uncompromising face, she had no difficulty in believing he meant what he said. She swallowed nervously, but refused to allow herself to be intimidated by him.

'Don't you think you're overdoing the great white protector bit? I have my own life and I'd like you to leave me alone to live it!'

His arms tightened, drawing her closer against him, his hard body an insinuation in itself, and her eyes flew to his face. 'You're not the type to live alone.' His eyes settled sensuously on her lips, the look a caress.

They were barely moving, but Alex's body burned where it touched his. Her heartbeats accelerated and when her lips trembled he smiled knowingly. 'You see,' he breathed, moving closer, his lips gently kissing her earlobe after moving feather-soft along the line of her jaw. 'I know you better than you know yourself. Your body will never forget mine, so why fight the inevitable?' His lips continued to nuzzle her earlobe, sending molten fire through her veins.

His hand slid down her back to settle around the swell of her hip, holding her closer. She knew she had to put some distance between them and pushed against his shoulder but, of course, he was too strong.

'Don't fight it, Alex.' His mouth found hers and then he raised his head, his own lips curving sensually.

Beneath her hand flat against his chest Alex felt his heartbeats quicken and she knew he was not as immune to her as he would like her to think he was. Drawing her back against him, he slid his lips down the column of her throat and his hold on her tightened urgently.

'Where are you staying?' he murmured.

'Blue Waters flats, around the corner from here,' she heard herself reply. 'It's a block of units that Chris owns.'

'What time do you finish?' His lips had returned to tease her earlobe.

'We're usually finished by two o'clock.'

'I'll be there,' he said thickly.

'No. No, I don't think you should,' Alex choked out, livid with herself for allowing him to find out so easily where she was staying. 'I don't want you to.'

He laughed huskily. 'You know you do. So why pretend?'

'I just . . . I share the flat,' she got out. 'It wouldn't be convenient.'

His eyes looked down into her face, narrowed, piercing into her very soul. 'Not convenient? For whom?'

'My . . . my flatmate,' she replied nervously.

'Well, make it convenient,' Justin said arrogantly. 'Surely it can be arranged,' he added drily, running his hand slowly up her spine, and she trembled responsively. 'Can't it, Alex?' His voice was low and provocative.

'No. No, Justin!' She pushed against him, taking him a little by surprise, so that his hands now rested on her waist and they were about a foot apart. 'Paul wouldn't understand,' she said clearly. 'Now I have to get back to work.'

His eyes raked her only once before he turned without a word and left her standing in among the other dancers.

CHAPTER SIX

WHEN the doorbell pealed next morning Alex almost ignored it, but curiosity got the better of her and she crossed to put her eye to the peephole in the door. Ben pulled a face and grinned at her and she opened the door and stood back for him to come in.

'Hi!' He stood in the living-room, his hands thrust into the back pockets of his dark jeans, his striped T-shirt moulding strong shoulders. 'I didn't know whether or not you'd be up, seeing as it's your day off.'

'I don't often sleep in.' Alex pushed a strand of fair hair back behind her ear. 'The weather's too nice to do that, I feel I shouldn't waste it. I usually go down to the beach.'

'But not today?'

'No, not today,' she said quietly. 'I have a few odd jobs to do, a couple of letters to write.'

'May I sit down?'

'Of course. I'm sorry, Ben.' Alex subsided into the chair opposite him. 'Would you like some coffee?'

'No, thanks.' His eyes moved about the flat. 'Not a bad place.' He stood up and walked to the sliding glass doors, and leant up against the door frame. 'Not a bad view.'

'Yes. Sitting out on the balcony there is another great temptation to time-wasting,' smiled Alex, wondering what Ben had to say that had him unsettled, and hoping it had nothing to do with Justin. Some hope, she mused tensely.

Ben sat down again, resting his elbows on his knees.

'Well, what do you think about being in the movie? Stick with me, kid,' he held an imaginary cigar between his fingers and moved his dark eyebrows up and down, 'I'm gonna make you a star.'

Alex laughed and shook her head.

'You aren't giving me the right amount of reverence, sweetie. Something tells me you're not exactly ecstatic about the idea.' He looked at her levelly.

'The boys are celebrating about it already. I . . .' Alex shrugged. 'I haven't any illusions, Ben. I guess I know I haven't got that certain something that makes a true star.'

Ben's eyes fell to his clasped hands. 'I would have said you had that and more six years ago.' He looked straight at her. 'What happened, Alex?'

'You know as well as I do what happened.' Alex ran a finger absently along the crease in her jeans. 'Raking it all up now won't change things.'

'I know, Alex. That's the last thing I want to do, but I care about both of you. See it from my side. Here you are looking all pale and lifeless and there's Justin in a permanent bad temper. You can't tell me you're both happier apart.'

'You've got it wrong there. We aren't happy together,' Alex retorted bitterly.

Ben sighed. 'Justin was livid with you last night after you made that impromptu announcement over the microphone.' He watched her stand up and prowl about the room before turning to look at him.

'It was accidental. Surely you can't imagine I said it on purpose?' He was looking back at his hands. 'Ben?'

'Well, I did wonder, Alex,' he said uncomfortably. 'We kind of turned it into something of a joke.' He watched her carefully for her reactions. 'Bindi Oliver was most sympathetic.' He grinned as Alex turned back

to him and he shrugged his shoulders. 'Bindi's that kind
of girl.'

Alex made no comment, but a familiar pain niggled
away inside her as she imagined those scarlet-tipped fingers on Justin's strong arm, those scarlet-tinted lips . . .
She turned abruptly away and didn't see the satisfied
expression cross her brother-in-law's face.

'If you still care about him, Alex, why don't you tell
him so?' Ben asked softly.

'I don't still care about him,' Alex snapped. 'It's been
over for six years and I've made another life for myself.
I definitely didn't want him turning up again.'

'You must have expected that he would one day.'

'Why should I have? A letter from his solicitor would
have done just as well.'

'You mean Justin's asked you for a divorce?' Ben
asked incredulously.

'No, not exactly in so many words.'

'Oh. For a minute I thought that's what had him all
worked up after you danced together last night. Even
Bindi couldn't get through to him. I guess you had
words about your—er—accidental announcement?' Ben
enquired.

'Can't we talk about something else, Ben?' Alex sat
down heavily in the chair she had been sitting in earlier.

'Okay, Alex. It's just that . . . Oh, hell! Pray that
Cupid's arrow gives me a miss!' He raised his hands,
then let them fall and changed the subject. 'Mum and
Dad are coming up to spend a couple of weeks with me,
with us, at the unit. They're flying up this evening. I
suppose Justin told you about Dad's heart attack. The
change should do them both good and the weather's
ideal at present.'

'They should enjoy it,' said Alex, wishing that fate
could have manipulated her to Darwin or Perth instead

of this particular place at this particular time. 'They'll be happy having the four of you back together again, if only for a couple of weeks.'

'I guess so. They'd be happier if it was the five of us,' he added, and Alex gave him an exasperated look. 'Perhaps we'd better talk about the film. I've arranged with Chris to talk to the four of you at Christie's on Wednesday morning. The lighting crew will be going over the place and we should be able to do the filming the week after.'

'It will only be singing, won't it, Ben? I mean, I won't have to learn lines or anything, will I?' frowned Alex.

'No, you just sing—and look beautiful,' he grinned. 'Nothing to it.' He glanced at his watch. 'Can I coax you out to have lunch with me?'

Alex hesitated.

'Just the two of us,' said Ben, knowing the reason for her dubiety. 'Justin had left for parts unknown by the time I woke this morning.'

'I didn't really think you'd try to contrive to get us together,' Alex began.

'Oh, yes, I would, Alex,' Ben hastened to put her right. 'I'd do it quick smart if I thought it would work. However, at this particular moment I'd say the odds were stacked against it being very successful. You two are the most stubborn . . .' He grimaced. 'Anyway, enough of that. How about that lunch? I'll even prepare it myself with these two capable hands. How does chicken salad sound? I'm famous for my tossed salads. My guests have tossed my salads left, right and centre,' he teased.

'Oh, Ben, you really are the limit!' Alex laughed. 'All right, give me a couple of minutes to change my clothes.'

The unit where Ben was staying was on the other side

of Surfers at a new subdivision called Paradise Waters and the whole building spelt luxury, from the carpeted foyer, up the silent elevator, to the hallway which gave entrance to the two units on the top floor. Ben told Alex that the other unit was leased by a Gold Coast businessman who was apparently away overseas at the moment. This fitted in very well for Ben as he felt he could have small parties without worrying about disturbing his neighbours.

Inside, it was all it promised to be. The living room was decorated in soft muted colours and Ben drew back the curtains so that Alex could admire the view over the Southport Broadwater, gleaming crystal blue in the sunshine, patterned by the hundreds of bobbing yachts and cruisers of all sizes, shapes and colours. The kitchen and dining areas were compact but comfortable, and two large bedrooms and a small study made up the rest of the unit.

For a while Alex expected Justin to walk in on them, but she gradually relaxed as she helped Ben prepare their lunch. They chatted companionably about Ben's movie and before they sat down at the smoked glass dining table Ben insisted on opening a bottle of wine to toast his latest film's success. By the time they were halfway through their meal they were laughing together without restraint the way they had always done when they first met.

Hundreds of surfers were taking advantage of the bright sunny weather as they swam in the blue surf, rode their surfboards on the white-crested waves or simply lay on the warm sand soaking up the sun. Nothing much could have been added to the scene to improve it, the miles of white beach stretching along the coast fringing the Pacific Ocean, its myriad colour tones through blue to green.

From his vantage point sitting on the low cement wall that separated the sandy beach from the footpath along the foreshore, Justin had an almost panoramic view of the entire beach. The white sand provided an ideal backdrop for the vibrant multi-colours of the beach umbrellas and beach towels. Tanned bodies glistened with suntan lotion, eyes shielded by dark glasses, noses starkly white smeared with protective zinc cream, and all the while the white-capped waves continued their undaunted assault upon the sand.

He wore his brief swim-shorts and had his towel slung carelessly across one tanned shoulder. The few hours he had spent body-surfing had toned up his muscles, shaken away some of the cobwebs caused by his sleepless night, and beneath the warmth of the sun he could feel the minute crystals of salt clinging to his now dry skin.

Behind his sunglasses his gaze subjected the beach and its occupants to another thorough appraisal. Once or twice his eyes hovered on a female figure, tall and fair-haired, but moved on when he had ascertained that it wasn't Alex. He had seen the three young men from her group down in the surf, but as far as he could tell Alex was not with them.

And even if she had been here what could they possibly have had to say to each other anyway? His bare toe absently scribed patterns in the patch of sand. For the two of them to sit down and have a rational conversation seemed an abject impossibility.

They only had to look at each other and it was daggers drawn. Until they touched. The familiar fire leapt within him and he cursed himself derisively. God, if she only knew how close he had come to . . . His jaw tensed until it ached. He genuinely could have killed her last night. 'I'm not interested in Justin de Wilde!' The words spun taunting through his mind and his lip curled. How he'd love to make her eat those words! And it would be so easy. No matter how much she protested to the contrary and no matter how many young men she shared her flat with, she was not as averse to him as she professed to be.

He bit off an angry retort and sprang agilely off the wall startling two elderly ladies who had stopped to watch the surfers. Striding across the road, he unlocked the door of his hire car and climbed behind the wheel. He drove around the block away from the main city shopping area and found the apartment block he was looking for without much trouble.

The letterboxes were inside the foyer and he ran his eye over the tenants. Chris Georgi, Apartment twenty. He strode purposefully towards the elevator and was soon standing at the door. The bell pealed for some time before he acknowledged that no one was inside.

The build-up of frustrated tension churned within him as he stood rigidly in the hallway and he had to determinedly fight down the almost overwhelming urge to thrust his fist through the door of the flat. Taking a deep calming breath, he turned away, part of him horrified at the ease with which he could be provoked into acting so out of character.

He sat in his car and taking a packet of cigarettes from the dashboard glovebox he flicked one out and lit up, forcing himself to relax, to try to get everything back into perspective. His muscles were tensed like coiled springs and he took a couple more deep breaths.

When he had first met Alex she had never reduced him to this state, turned him inside out the way she had done since he had watched her as she sat singing her songs at the restaurant in Brisbane. He felt like a dog chasing his tail, forever turning in a futile circle.

On that particular afternoon in the sunny King George Square when she had cannoned into him and his life, he had had no premonition of what was to come. Physically he was attracted to her and he remembered the surge of success when he had convinced her to share a conversation over a cup of coffee. He knew she had been hesitant about accepting.

The cup of coffee had stretched into three cups apiece, and all the while they had talked. Despite her youth Alex had spoken with shy but intelligent common sense, and Justin found himself totally interested in her. Never before could he remember having such a feeling of unity with a woman—well, she was barely a woman.

And her youth had worried him a little in the beginning. He knew she was not a typically modern girl and although she mentioned a few young men in conversation he doubted very much if any of her relationships had been other than friendship. That thought had put a tight rein on him, but after their lips had met in their first kiss, everything had ceased to exist for them except each other.

Who would have thought it would have ended so disastrously? Her parents and his parents, his mother especially, had been against their marriage. His mother had made no bones about her opposition. There were too many years between them and their backgrounds were so very different.

Maybe they had rushed headlong into it—he sighed—but it had all seemed so right somehow. At least, he had been incapable of stopping it and he had had no desire to anyway.

After their conversation in the coffee shop he had called to take Alex out every night he was free during the two weeks he was in Brisbane. They went to dinner, to live theatre, to the movies and to the Folk Centre where Alex often sang. He could recall vividly that last night with the clarity of his heightened senses.

Until that night he had succeeded in keeping their relationship on a purely platonic level. Oh, he had been aware that each time they inadvertently touched they had both known that the river of a physical attraction flowed very close to the surface, but he kept telling himself that he was twelve years her senior, that they were two people who had met in passing, who could enjoy each other's company for a short time and then part.

Sitting in the warm car, he drew deeply on his cigarette and slowly exhaled. He smirked derisively at the cigarette end. So much for his good intentions! That last evening began as any other evening they had shared began. They went to a well-known seafood restaurant down in the Valley and they danced and talked. In those days they had never ceased to find a topic of mutual interest. And as they danced their eyes were drawn to each other and the awareness between them intensified.

Eventually he had dropped Alex home at her parents' house and, reluctant to bring the evening to an end, he had accepted her offer of a cup of coffee. The house was in darkness and he followed her along the path and unlocked the door for her.

They went through to the kitchen and he stood watching her as she busied herself heating the water, setting out the coffee mugs. He asked after her parents and as she led him through to the living-room she told him a little warily that they were away for the weekend. For the first time their conversation became a trifle stilted, and as Alex sat on the edge of her chair sipping her coffee, he could almost see the nervous flutter of her heart. The air between them had crackled and in all honesty he knew he was as keyed up as she was trying hard to hide she was.

'When are you leaving?' she had asked him at last.

'Tomorrow morning.' Justin looked down into the dark liquid in his cup. 'I've got solid commitments for two weeks, then I'll have a few days' break before the next lot of engagements in the far north—Cairns, Townsville, Mount Isa.'

She nodded, a curtain of silky hair falling forward, and she brushed it carefully back from her face. 'Have you been up to northern Queensland before?'

'No. My first time,' he smiled. 'Everyone I've spoken to either loves it or hates it. I'm really quite curious to see it for myself.'

An uneasy silence settled on them for a few moments and he watched her dart a quick glance at him through her lashes before concentrating on the coffee mug in her hands.

'Would you like another cup of coffee?' she asked, and he wondered if it was a trick of the light that her lips had seemed to take on a whitish hue.

'No, thanks.' He rose and put his empty mug on the coffee table. 'I guess I should be going. I've an early flight.' His fingers straightened his tie and putting her own coffee cup down Alex stood up facing him.

'I hope you have a good flight, and thanks so much for tonight, for the last two weeks. I've really enjoyed your company.' She walked across to the door and her hand was on the catch before Justin moved after her.

'I've enjoyed it, too, Alex,' he said softly, and meant it.

She smiled faintly. 'I'm glad.' She held out her hand and her smile widened. 'Don't forget to call in again when you're passing through Brisbane.'

His eyes seemed to be compelled to move over her face, settling on the gentle curve of her lips before he pulled himself together and took the hand she offered

him. Once her hand was in his he found he didn't want
to let it go, and when she would have taken her hand
away he held it captive. Her smile faltered and a rosy
flush touched her cheeks. She raised startled blue eyes
from the knot of his tie to meet his own eyes.

How long they stood like that he couldn't have told,
but only the slightest pressure brought her up against
him and releasing her hand he slid his arms around her,
holding her close. It seemed that both their bodies sighed
as though they had been existing simply for this
moment.

His eyes never left her face as he drank in each of her
features—her small upturned nose, her wide deep violet
eyes, the perfectly shaped lips now trembling slightly.

'Alex?' The name came huskily from him in a voice
he scarcely recognised as his own, before he lowered his
head.

That long kiss was an explosion within them both,
left them both shaken and unfulfilled. When they finally
drew apart their eyes locked together as they drew
ragged breaths. But not for long. Their lips were lured
irresistibly together. Alex moaned softly as Justin's lips
moved down the smooth column of her throat and he
felt his control slip dangerously low.

How they ended up on the couch he barely recalled,
but the feel of her lithe young body along the length of
his drove any of his earlier restraints to the furthermost
corner of his mind. Her satin blouse was soon loose of
the band of her long hostess skirt and his hands caressed
the rising swell of her young breasts. Her hands were
moving inside his shirt over the firmness of his midriff
and back, and they clung together in a feverish arousal.

He kissed her eyes, her nose, her mouth, the softness
of her throat, until his lips moved downwards and she
murmured in response, her fingers in the thick darkness

of his hair. Raising his head, he met her eyes again, the fire surging within him at the luminous sensuality he had drawn into their blue depths. Through the haze of his own heightened passion he also noticed that her eyes were tinged just slightly with a faint fear she was unable to hide from him, and he belatedly remembered her youth and inexperience and cursed himself for his selfish lack of control. Almost savagely he thrust himself to his feet, his hands unsteady as he began rebuttoning his shirt.

'Justin?'

'We . . .' He took a deep breath. 'We have to stop this, Alex. Otherwise I won't be able to.'

He put more distance between them as Alex struggled into a sitting position, blushing as she pulled her blouse together. He turned back to her when he felt he had regained some of his control, and the look in her eyes, of pain, of uncertainty, was almost his undoing.

He leant stiff-armed against the back of the lounge chair, and stared at the whiteness of his tensed knuckles. God, how he wanted her! His eyes went to her again. 'Don't look at me like that, Alex, or, God help me, I won't be able to keep this distance between us,' he said harshly.

'I'm sorry,' she whispered. 'I'm afraid I don't under-stand how . . .' She stopped and began again. 'I mean, I guess I'm not very experienced about . . . I've never . . .' Her voice faded away and Justin clenched his hands before he could trust himself to speak.

'I know, Alex, I know. That's why I don't want to . . .' He looked back at her. 'Alex. Oh, Alex!' He ran his hands through his hair and stared broodingly at her. 'I love you and I want to marry you,' he said at last, and her mouth opened in a round oh of shocked surprise as she continued to stare at him.

His hand moved tiredly over his jaw. 'Hell, I've made a mess of this,' he said almost to himself, and sighed. 'Look, I think we could use another cup of coffee before we talk about it. Okay?'

Nodding, Alex slowly got to her feet and picked up the two coffee mugs. Her eyes were downcast, as though she was afraid to look at him.

Leaning in the doorway, his arms folded, Justin watched as she made the coffee, his eyes narrowed, his thoughts concealed. Her face was turned away from him, her hair falling in slight disarray from their love-making, and he knew the rekindling of his arousal. Before he could stop himself he had crossed the kitchen to slide his arms around her from behind, drawing her easily back against him, his hands going to the swell of her breasts, burying his face in the softness of her hair.

'Oh, Alex,' he breathed, 'I knew this would happen.'

'What ... what would happen?' she asked breathlessly, a catch in her voice.

'That if I touched you I wouldn't be able to leave you alone.' His lips gently caressed her neck and he felt her tremble. Turning her around, his hands moved to cup her face. 'I mean what I say, Alex, make no mistake about that. This is no light flirtation for me. I do want to marry you.'

Tears spilled over on to her cheeks and her arms slid around his waist. 'I love you, too. I wouldn't have been able to bear it if you'd simply left tonight.'

He kissed her gently on the mouth and they stood together smiling at each other. He sighed and rested his head against hers. 'Mmm, what a night! Let's have that coffee. We've got plans to make.'

They were married two weeks later and spent a three-day honeymoon on Green Island out from Cairns before his next group of engagements began. Those first months of their marriage had been ideal, and if anyone had told Justin their marriage would have broken apart within six short months he would have laughed in disbelief.

So much for perfect bliss! He stubbed out his cigarette and after a last look at the block of units he started the car and turned in the direction of Paradise Waters. As he drove along he found himself once again analysing his relationship with Alex. Surely after all that had passed he should be able to put her behind him. Why did she still have the power to take his ordered restrained way of life and wipe aside the civilised principles he thought had been second nature to him? What was the hold she had over him?

When he was apart from her all he could think about were the clear serenity of her eyes, the tilt of her chin, the sway of her body. And yet when they were together they circled each other like wary antagonists preparing to make the first hit. His knuckles were white on the steering wheel and he forced his hands to relax.

Parking his car under the block of units, he grimaced as he walked past Ben's car on his way to the elevator, wishing irrationally that Ben was away filming and hoping fervently that his brother wasn't entertaining any of his arty friends. To be civil to them at present would take a huge effort on his part, and besides, he'd really like to shut himself in his room and lose himself in some paperwork he'd brought along with him. He needed the oblivion of fierce concentration to take his mind from Alex.

His sandalled footsteps were lost in the thick pile of the carpet and he stopped in front of the door, flipping through his key case for the right key. When he opened the door the sound of laughter bubbled into the hallway and he sighed in irritation. At least he could use the fact that he needed to shower and change as an excuse to pass through the living-room without lingering.

The door closed behind him with a decisive click and as he strode forward he noticed that the laughter had stopped. By the time he had rounded the partition dividing the living-room from the dining-room the couple seated at the table had turned towards him, Ben's expression guarded while Alex's mirrored a shocked dismay.

To come upon Alex sitting in the unit with Ben took him so much by surprise that he paused in mid-stride and found he had difficulty catching his breath. Recovering quickly, he advanced, face set, into the room, angry with himself, with Ben and with Alex.

CHAPTER SEVEN

THE sound of the closing of Ben's front door had not immediately filled Alex with apprehension. Ben's company and her unaccustomed glass of white wine in the middle of the day had relaxed her and she was thoroughly enjoying herself. Therefore when Justin appeared she was taken completely aback. Surprise at once turned to anger that he should continually crop up when she least expected him, before she could steal herself to his appearance.

Ben seemed to be the first to recover himself. 'Justin! Hi! We're in the middle of lunch. Come and join us.'

'Thanks, Ben, I will. Hello, Alex.' His eyes watched as she looked down at her fingers, nervously crumbling her bread roll. 'Give me a couple of minutes to shower and change.' He strolled through to his room, leaving a heavy silence behind him.

'Alex, I'm sorry,' said Ben earnestly. 'I really didn't know he was coming back for lunch, believe me.'

'I know,' Alex sighed. 'I guess we'll just have to make the best of it.'

'That's the spirit,' Ben grinned. 'You should simply try to treat each other as friends.'

Alex gave a short laugh.

'Well, Bindi and Tony were once married to each other. They've been divorced over a year and they're still the best of friends.'

Alex was surprised by this piece of information, but she shook her head, not being able to see herself and Justin in the same situation. They could never be friends, there was too much antagonism between them, and she said as much to Ben.

'There doesn't have to be, does there?' he asked seriously. 'Can't you forget about the past and at least be civil to each other?'

Alex shook her head. 'I don't know, Ben. I'm so confused. I loved Justin desperately, blindly—maybe that was the trouble, and when he . . . Well, it really crushed me.' She grimaced. 'The idol had feet of clay.'

'Justin wouldn't have professed to be a god. He never wanted you to look at him in that light. No man would.'

'Perhaps not.' She sighed again. 'I guess my parents were right all the time, and your parents, too. I should never have married him,' she said flatly.

Ben's eyes went from her face to a point behind her shoulders and with a shiver of apprehension she realised that they were no longer alone. That Justin had over-heard her quiet words was written all over the pale tenseness of his face as he sat down at the table.

'I'll freshen up the coffee,' said Ben, standing up. 'Help yourself to the wine, Justin. Alex and I have sampled it and we can recommend it, can't we, sweetie?' Ben gave her an audacious wink before turning back to the kitchenette.

In silence Justin poured his wine, holding it up to the light, twisting the stem of the glass in his strong fingers while Alex could only watch him, her breathing shallow and laboured, her heartbeats fluttering out of time. Just as the silence was becoming unbearable he turned his cold eyes on her and took a slow deliberate sip of his wine.

'Well, Alex, you do manage to turn up in the most unexpected places.'

She was immediately on the defensive. 'Ben was kind

enough to bring me here for lunch,' she began.

His smile didn't even come near his eyes. 'Yes, Ben is very kind, aren't you, Ben?' He turned to his brother, who grinned unconcernedly at the cold steel lying barely covered in his brother's tone.

'Kindness itself, that's me.' He sat down and poured the freshly brewed coffee. 'Eat up, Justin. There's plenty left.'

'Thank you,' Justin replied drily, heaping green salad on to the plate Ben set down in front of him.

'I've mentioned to Alex that the folks are arriving later this afternoon.' Ben added sugar to his coffee. 'I'm looking forward to seeing them. I've been away for the past five or six months,' he explained for Alex's benefit, 'and with Dad having that attack I worry about him a bit. Mum has the devil of a job keeping him from over-doing it.'

'Did . . . did the attack leave him with any permanent damage?' Alex asked, not looking at Justin.

'No. He was really lucky. Gave him and us one hell of a scare at the time.' Ben shook his head. 'He seemed so well, too. He loves his gardening.'

Alex smiled. 'Remember the time that young fellow from down the street had a few too many drinks and cut some of Dad's roses? He was so mad!'

Ben laughed with her. 'Do I ever! He thought I'd done it for a while. Took me ages to convince him I was absolutely innocent. Remember that, Justin?' He tried to include his brother in the conversation.

'Can't say I do,' Justin replied, refilling his wine glass.

'I think it was while Justin was away in New Zealand,' Alex ventured.

'Could have been, too,' Ben nodded. 'I must re-member to remind Dad about it.'

They spent the next half hour or so reminiscing. Or,

at least, Alex and Ben did. Justin added little to the conversation and Alex became alarmed at the number of times he topped up his wine glass.

'Why don't you come with us to the airport to pick up the folks?' Ben's words caught her attention again. 'They'd love to see you, wouldn't they, Justin? Especially Dad.'

'Oh, Ben, no!' Alex spoke quickly, horrified at the thought of facing Mrs de Wilde without warning. 'I'd better not. I think it would probably be best if you two go along as arranged.'

For a moment it seemed as though Ben would try to change her mind, but one look at his brother's unsmiling face made him nod acquiescence. 'Okay, then. But you'll have to have dinner with us one evening, won't she, Justin?'

'Of course.' His tone was not encouraging.

Alex glanced at her watch. 'I . . . I should be getting along, Ben,' she appealed to him. Much more of this one-sided conversation and she'd go mad!

'Right. I'll drive you back.' Ben pushed back his chair.

'I'll take Alex home,' said Justin, firmly setting his knife and fork on his plate, leaving his lunch barely touched.

'Oh, it's all right. Ben can . . .' Alex began, but the jangle of the telephone cut across her protest.

Ben reached across the breakfast bar as Alex's eyes flicked away from Justin's. If he thought she was going to . . .

'Ben de Wilde.' Ben listened for a moment before pulling a face at Alex and motioning that he would be some time and that she should go with Justin.

'Come on.' Justin took her arm and led her towards the living-room as Ben waved and mouthed that he would see her on Wednesday.

In the confined space of the elevator Alex kept as much distance between them as was possible, her eyes downcast, with only the legs of his faded denim flares and the casual sandals on his feet in her line of vision. Once her eyes moved involuntarily upwards over the muscular hardness of his thighs and she felt herself shiver at the memories that her mind flashed before her.

Out of the elevator he strode across and opened the door of a green Ford Fairlaine, standing back for Alex to get into the passenger seat.

Alex hesitated. 'Look, Justin, there's no need for you to take me back. I can easily catch a taxi.'

'Get in, Alex. It's not far to your flat.'

'I . . . I was going to the beach.'

'Then I'll take you to the beach,' he said distinctly. 'Just get in. Or do you want me to help you in?'

'I simply didn't want to put you to the trouble,' said Alex as she moved past him and climbed into the car with ill grace.

He glared at her as he closed the door and walked around to the driver's side, while Alex wished she had the nerve to climb out of the car and make her escape.

'Which beach?' he asked as the engine roared to life.

'Surfers, thank you.'

'Do you need to collect your swimsuit first?'

'No. I have my bikini on underneath my dress,' she replied.

Nothing more was said until Justin turned out on to the highway. Alex realised her fingers were playing nervously with her seatbelt and clasped her hands firmly in her lap.

'How did you come to be lunching with Ben?' he asked.

Feeling irrationally put out that he should question

her, Alex was unable to keep the sharpness, the aggression, out of her voice. 'He called at the flat to talk to me about the film and as it was lunchtime he asked me to share a meal with him. Why?'

Justin moved his shoulders slightly. 'Just curious. I expected you to be at the beach.'

'I had a few things to do this morning.' There was another brief silence. 'I thought you were holidaying on the Barrier Reef somewhere.' The words slipped out before Alex could bite them back. The last thing she wanted to do was give him reason to suspect she was interested in his whereabouts.

'I was,' he replied carefully, 'but I decided to join Ben down here.'

'Your parents will be happy to see you.' Alex made what she thought was an unprovocative remark.

'Undoubtedly.' His lip curled cynically. 'But not you.'

'Me?' Alex spoke quickly, flushing slightly at his implication. 'I can't see what I've got to do with it.'

He turned the car left and then right on to the beachfront. 'Can't you, Alex?' he asked softly.

'You can drop me off anywhere along here,' she said ignoring the sensual tone of his last words, sighing with relief that their journey had ended.

He pulled easily into the first vacant parking space and switched off the engine, following her out on to the footpath and locking the doors behind him.

Alex's nerves stretched to high pitch as he straightened and pocketed his keys. 'Thanks for the lift,' she began, her tone dismissing.

'Don't mention it,' he said, falling into step beside her.

Frowning, Alex stopped, turning to face him, ready to do battle, but he took her arm and set her moving again.

'I'll join you in a surf,' he said. 'Like you, I have my bathers on underneath.'

'You don't have to do that,' Alex said tersely.

'Oh, but I want to.' His tone was smooth, amiable.

'You don't seem to understand, Justin. I don't want to go surfing with you,' Alex told him plainly.

He made no comment as he slipped off his sandals and waited for her to do likewise. 'What's so bad about swimming with me, Alex?'

She glanced up at the tone in his voice. She had expected a biting tirade, and now, here he was almost teasing.

'Afraid to?' He lifted one dark eyebrow quizzically.

'Of course I'm not afraid to go swimming with you. It's a public beach. It's just that I'm meeting the boys. I said I'd go swimming with them.' Alex stretched the truth a little. The plan was that she would see the others at the beach if she felt like it. In actual fact, it was the last thing she felt like doing, but she had no one to blame but herself for getting into the situation.

Justin's eyes were screwed up against the sun's glare and he took his dark glasses out of his pocket and put them on, shielding his expression still further. 'Then let's all go swimming together,' he said blithely.

Alex scanned the beach for the boys and she caught sight of Paul's lime green surfboard first. He'd stuck it into the sand and was stretched out, leaning his back against it. His face, pink from the sun, his nose sticky white with protective zinc cream, lit up when Alex's shadow fell on him, attracting his attention, and he called a welcome.

'About time, Alex. We'd given you up.' He stopped speaking when he noticed that Alex wasn't alone. 'Hi!' he added a little reluctantly.

Justin nodded.

'You must be holidaying on the Coast, I take it, Mr
de Wilde?' Paul's eyes flicked from Alex to Justin.

'Yes, I am.' Justin's smile took the younger man
aback. 'Make it Justin, Paul. No, I couldn't believe my
good luck when I realised Alex would be down here at
the moment as well.' He turned an enigmatic expression
on Alex's astounded face, while Paul's face turned even
pinker.

Alex's anger rose. So that was his game. Well, she'd
see about that!

'You flatter me, Mr de Wilde,' she said, almost offen-
sively. 'I'm sure you say that to every female singer.'
She fluttered her eyelashes in his direction.

'No, not every one. Only you, Alex.' He used her
christian name pointedly, looking straight at her, smiling charmingly.

To Alex's consternation her colour rose and she tried
to shrug nonchalantly. 'Yes, well, that remains to be
seen.' She turned back to Paul. 'Can I borrow your
surfboard for half an hour or so, love?'

If the endearment tacked on the end of her request
took Paul by surprise he didn't show any outward sign
that he was aware of it and he sat up and smiled at her.
'Sure. Take it for as long as you like.'

Without glancing at Justin Alex slipped out of her
blouse and undid the tie of her wraparound skirt before
picking up the fibreglass board and walking towards
the surf. She could feel Justin's eyes on her back and
didn't relax until she had paddled past the first line of
breakers.

The surf was reasonably high with the rather stiff
breeze whipping up the waves, and Alex was soon lost
in the exhilaration of cutting along the crest of a wave.
She wasn't overly confident about her ability at the

sport, but thanks to Paul's coaching she could stand on a board without toppling off into the water.

The wind caught her hair as she altered the position of her feet on the board to adjust the trim. Feeling the power going out of the wave, she moved to the tail of the board, swinging her forward foot up in the air and over the curl, catching the board as she cut through the back of the wave.

Sitting relaxedly astride the board waiting for another wave she considered she could tackle, Alex found her thoughts straying back to Justin with disturbing clarity. Why did he have to keep turning up to upset her, throw her off balance? And why should he make such a show of appearing interested in her in front of Paul? Surely he wouldn't stoop to being a dog in the manger?

Something soft touched her foot as it dangled in the blue water and she stifled a cry of fright, her first thoughts flashing the word shark. But even as she drew her feet out of the water and on to the board a tanned arm reached out and Justin was shaking the salt water out of his hair. He looked up at her, his eyes bright and clear, and gave her a mock salute.

'Permission to come aboard?'

'You're joking!' Alex let her feet slide back into the water, holding the edges of the board to steady it against Justin's off-centre weight. 'And you frightened the living daylights out of me. I thought it was a shark.'

'Perhaps you would have welcomed the shark more,' he said with a smile. The board lurched and he was sitting on the front, and Alex slid backwards to try to counterbalance his weight.

'Stay there. It should hold us both as long as we don't get too energetic.' He raised one eyebrow. 'When did you learn to board-ride?'

'Paul taught me a few months ago. I'm no expert, but

I manage if I don't have to do anything fancy.'

'How about teaching me?' he asked.

Alex looked at him, trying not to let her gaze fall down the tanned muscular length of his body. 'I wouldn't have thought surfboard riding was your thing at all.'

'I may surprise you.'

'Well, I couldn't teach anyone. I'm not sure enough of it all myself as yet,' Alex shrugged, 'so I guess you won't have to put yourself to the test.'

'Pity. It could have been fun. We may even have ended up friends.'

Alex raised her eyebrows.

'You'd be amazed at the ends to which I'll go to get what I want,' he said quietly.

'And what do you really want, Justin?'

'I told you, Alex. I want you back.'

'Why?' Alex kept her voice expressionless.

'Why wouldn't I? I repeat, you underestimate your attraction, Alex. You always did.' He leaned forward and ran one finger down her bare arm, his eyes resting on her tanned body. 'You look great in that bikini. No wonder Denman hangs around you, ever hopeful. You still haven't lost that quality you always had, to make a fellow feel he's straining at the leash but not quite able to reach out and touch you.' He shook his head. 'I used to feel the same way. But I've touched you, Alex. And I want to go on touching you.'

'I don't care to hear any more of that, Justin.' Alex's pulses raced and her skin burned where his finger trailed down her arm, and, angry with herself for her reactions to him, she retorted, 'Get off my board, please. I want to go ashore.'

'You're running away, Alex, from me and from yourself. What's the point? You can't run for ever.' His hand wrapped around her wrist. 'Stay and face it. Talk about it. I think we can find that bond we had if you'll only give it a chance.' His thumb almost absently rubbed the inside of her palm.

'You never give up, do you? For some misguided reason you suddenly want to pick up again after years of nothing. Well, it's no go! I have my own life now and it doesn't include you, so don't you think you should practise what you preach and face up to a few things yourself?'

'Alex, don't push me,' he said harshly, his fingers tightening, punishing her wrist.

'I wouldn't dare. Not the great Justin de Wilde, whose word is the law,' she replied sarcastically, looking at him scornfully.

His eyes bored into hers for immeasurable seconds before he threw her hand away from him and, using a word Alex had never before heard in polite conversation, he slipped off the surfboard and struck out for the beach.

Alex sat watching his dark head until tears blurred her vision. With the back of her hand she dashed them angrily from her eyes, chastising herself for her weakness. She'd wanted him to go, hadn't she? So why, all of a sudden, did she want him back so desperately, to take her in his arms and hold her close the way he used to do?

Well, there was no point in sitting out here wallowing in self-pity over a situation she'd brought on herself. All she had to do was tell him she was willing to make another attempt at their marriage and she could be back where she left off. But no, things could never be the same again. She was no longer the gauche young girl so blinded by her image of love and how it should be. Now she had grown up and all those pure girlish dreams were far behind her. She had reached maturity the hard way and she was incapable of wiping out the pain of these past six years. The crevasse ran too deep and throbbed too rawly to be so lightly, so easily plastered over. And who could pinpoint the moment when the first fracture had occurred? It would have been so easy to blame Margot for the first chink in their break-up, but Margot had only been a small part of it. A very small part. She could have coped with the situation if it had only been another woman, but . . .

Justin had not exaggerated when he said their troubles had begun when they returned to Sydney, and Alex had a terrible suspicion that a great deal of their troubles had been of her own making. If she had not been so young, so naïve, so unrealistic, almost dreamlike in her outlook then perhaps none of it would have happened. Maybe the twelve years' difference in their ages had been more important than they thought. Justin was a man of the world, while she had led a sheltered life all wrapped up in her dreams of how things should be.

Their few days' honeymoon on tropical Green Island had been pure bliss and perhaps had only encouraged Alex's fairytale view of life. The sky and sea were blue, the sand white, the trees green, and their lovemaking had been so much more earthshattering than Alex had ever dreamed it could be. It was as though they were the only two people on earth, wrapped totally in each other. The rest of the world was merely a backdrop for their existence.

No two people could have been happier and there had been no premonition of the turmoil to come. Alex had accompanied Justin as he continued his engagements in Northern Queensland and that had simply been a continuation of their shared days on the island.

Then in no time at all they were flying back to Sydney

and the first inkling that all might not be well had crept into the glowing aura of happiness that Alex had wrapped about her. At the thought of meeting Justin's parents for the first time her stomach had churned with nervousness. Just before their wedding she had spoken to them on the telephone and the impersonality of the instrument had made them all sound rather stilted and forced. It meant so much to her that she should make a good impression, have them like her.

And Justin's attitude had done nothing to dispel her nervousness. Since the evening before he had been quiet, loath to talk, less attentive, and over breakfast he had appeared to forget completely that she was there. On the plane he had closed his eyes and to all outward appearances he was catching up on some sleep while Alex sat beside him, wishing he would hold her hand or smile reassuringly at her.

In fact they were in a taxi heading towards the de Wilde home before she summoned up the courage to talk to him about her nervous reluctance at the coming meeting with his parents.

'I hope they like me.' She had to repeat it twice before he turned to her.

'They will,' he replied flatly, and returned his gaze to the passing suburbs through the window of the taxi.

'Justin, what's the matter?' she asked softly, her hand on his arm, over-conscious of the taxi driver in the front seat.

'Nothing's the matter. What could be?' he said then, lifting her hand and kissing it gently, a half smile on his face, and everything was almost all right again.

The taxi driver deposited their cases on the front porch of a very nice two-storey house, and Alex stood waiting while Justin paid their fare and stepped up to ring the doorbell.

Grace de Wilde opened the door herself, tall, poised, unsmiling, and at that first glance Alex could remember the sinking feeling of disquiet as her nervousness tripled. How would she ever be able to approach this self-possessed, elegant woman?

'Mother.' Justin stepped forward to put his arms lightly around her, kissing her on the cheek before turning to draw Alex up beside him. 'Mother, this is Alex.'

'How do you do, Alex.' Justin's mother touched her cheek briefly to Alex's. 'Come on inside.'

They sat in the living-room and drank tea from an exquisite bone china tea set and tried to talk. Sitting on the edge of her chair, Alex could only answer Justin or his mother in monosyllables, and she almost gasped with relief when Grace suggested that Justin show Alex to their room so that she could freshen up before dinner. Justin's father would be home by then.

Inside the room they were to share Alex sagged tiredly back against the closed door, feeling tears of despair well up in her eyes. 'Oh, Justin, she doesn't like me at all,' she cried to his back as he lifted her suitcase on to the bed.

'Don't be silly, Alex. Mother's only just met you. There's no reason why she'd take an instant dislike to you.' He turned and shoved his hands in the pockets of his trousers a frown on his face.

Tears tumbled down her pale cheeks and he crossed to her, pulling her gently against him. 'Alex, no tears. You're overtired.' He kissed her nose. 'I love you, and when she gets to know you, so will Mother. Why not have a shower and lie down for a while? You'll feel better when you've rested.'

Alex nodded slowly. 'What . . . what will you do?'

'I'll go down and chat to Mother. She likes to hear all about my tours. Now, off you go. I'll come up and get you in good time for dinner.' He kissed her softly again and left her.

After a relaxing shower and rest Alex did feel better and she dressed for dinner with special care, choosing a pale blue crêpe dress, its simple lines accentuating her slim figure, the pale blue colour highlighting the clear blue of her eyes. She brushed her hair until it shone and she was applying just a light touch of make-up when Justin returned.

'Ready, love?'

Alex stood back from the mirror. 'Yes. Just about.'

'Feel better now?' he asked softly, sounding more like he had in the first weeks of their marriage.

'Mmm, much better.' Alex nodded. 'Do I look all right?'

Justin's eyes moved over her in a proprietorial fashion, the flame leaping there bringing a flush to her cheeks. 'You look beautiful. I think we'd best go down right away, before my ideas develop any further.' He took her arm, his fingers moving slowly over her firm bare skin.

Justin's father arrived home as Justin and Alex descended the stairs and he smiled up at them with Justin's smile. Alex relaxed, taking to him immediately. He kissed her soundly, congratulating his son on his choice of brides and welcoming Alex to the family. Everything was going to be all right. Maybe Justin had been right, she had been simply tired.

Grace de Wilde joined them and suggested they go into the living-room for a drink before dinner. And it was as they sat over their meal that Alex heard Margot's name mentioned for the first of many times.

'Did you know Margot was back from Europe?' Grace asked her son.

Justin shook his head, his expression not changing as he sipped his wine.

'Yes, we met in the city for lunch last week. She'll most probably be working with you again this season.' Grace turned to Alex. 'Margot's a fine soprano and an old friend of Justin's. You'll have heard of her? Margot Donald.'

'No. I'm afraid I haven't,' Alex replied. 'I . . . I'm not very familiar with classical musicians.'

'Oh.' There seemed to Alex to be a wealth of meaning in that one short word, and her new-found confidence ebbed quickly away.

'Justin told us you play the guitar and sing yourself,' John de Wilde put in.

'Only for my own enjoyment,' Alex hurriedly informed them. 'I play mainly folk songs and ballads.'

'Alex sings, or should I say, sang regularly at the Folk Centre in Brisbane,' added Justin.

'Did you do that for your living?' asked Grace, making Alex feel like a dance hall girl.

'Oh, no,' she said quickly. 'I've been studying at the Uni.'

'I see.'

Alex shrank inside herself. Whatever Justin's mother saw wasn't a favourable picture, if her expression was any indication of her thoughts.

'Alex is now going to be studying full-time,' Justin laughed into the heavy atmosphere. 'She'll be studying looking after me.'

His father laughed with him. 'That will be a full-time job if I know Justin! You'll have your work cut out for you. Still, it's a refreshing change to see a young woman who's content to take on the mammoth task of being a good wife and mother.'

'Only a wife for the time being.' Justin smiled as Alex flushed. 'I want her all to myself for a while.' He squeezed Alex's hand.

'And here I'd set my heart on being a grandfather quite soon,' chuckled Justin's father.

'Well, you could always talk to Ben,' suggested Justin, his eyes twinkling.

'Ben's too busy,' said his father. 'No. My hopes rest with you and Alex.'

'Really, John,' Grace broke in, 'it's hardly your business. And as Justin said, they are only recently married.'

'We had Justin within the year,' reminded her husband, not daunted by his wife's reproving look.

'Yes, well, things were different then.' She lifted the coffee pot. 'More coffee, Justin?'

The following few weeks they stayed with Justin's parents, and while Justin and his father were there Alex found it bearable. However, they were both away for most of the day. Justin had to recommence rehearsals and commuted to the city each day with his father. This left Alex with Grace, and for Alex the days were long and strained.

Alex found it almost impossible to talk to Justin's mother without feeling like a gauche schoolgirl. The older woman seemed indifferent to Alex as her daughter-in-law was unable to discuss Grace's pet subject, classical music, in any depth. In fact, neither seemed to be able to relax with the other.

When they did talk Alex began to grow aware of the number of times Margot Donald's name came into the conversation, and Alex became increasingly curious about her.

However, it wasn't until she moved with Justin to his apartment in the city that she actually met Margot.

Two weeks after their arrival in Sydney Justin's brother came home, and to a degree he was Alex's salvation. Ben was the one person Alex could talk to without restraint. She could relax completely with Ben, and be herself. They always seemed to laugh together, a fact which appeared to irritate Grace de Wilde even more.

When Justin flew to New Zealand he decided that the trip of hectic engagements was best done alone, and as Alex faced the ten days without him with horror Ben turned up to take her sightseeing. Alex could barely hide her relief.

They left the house early in the mornings like two children on a promised outing and returned late at night tired and happy. In fact they were out the afternoon Justin arrived back in Sydney. He had managed to catch an earlier flight and rang from the airport for Alex to meet him and stay in town for dinner. Finding Alex out, Justin decided to stay at his apartment and return home the next day as planned.

Alex and Ben had dined out themselves and a bottle of wine had relaxed Alex to the point where she began to giggle when Ben had trouble inserting his key in the lock. The door opened and Grace de Wilde faced them, her expression relegating them both to wayward children. One more black mark, Alex tallied up.

Then when Ben went off to film on location in Adelaide Alex's days fell back into the strained co-existence she shared with her mother-in-law until Justin arrived home one night to find Alex pale and drawn, her eyes red with crying, and suggested she come up to the apartment where they could stay for a week or so to give her a change of scene.

Although he would be busy with rehearsals, Alex jumped at the chance. Anything to relieve the yawning emptiness of the days stretching ahead without him. At least they could have the nights together and Alex would have the opportunity to cook for him. At his parents' home Grace rarely allowed Alex to do anything. Once she had made their bed and tidied their room there was very little left for her to do but wait for Justin's return for dinner.

Their first night at the small apartment Alex spent all afternoon preparing their dinner. She worked happily, singing to herself, anticipating the evening ahead. By the time Justin arrived home she had the small dining room table nicely set, candles glowing, and their favourite wine chilled in an ice bucket. He smiled at the table and slipped out of his jacket his eyes moving over her.

'Mmm,' he sighed, his arms pulling her to him. 'I feel better already. Have I got time for a shower?'

Alex slid her arms about him and nodded, kissing the firm curve of his jawline. 'It's so good to have you to myself,' she whispered.

'You realise, Mrs de Wilde, that you're going to have to take the consequences of all this romance,' he murmured against her ear.

'I hope that's a promise, Mr de Wilde,' Alex laughed softly, and his arms tightened. His kiss arched Alex against him and he groaned and held her away from him. 'Alex, you're a witch! Much more of that and your dinner will be absolutely ruined!' He released her reluctantly and disappeared into the bedroom.

Their meal was a huge success and they slipped back into the togetherness they had shared in the first weeks of their marriage. By the time they retired to the living-room with their coffee, the lights low, soft music adding to the mood, a glow of excitement had caught Alex in its web, righting her world again, wiping out the past weeks. Justin drew her on to his knee, kissing the softness of her throat.

'Mmm, it's wonderful being by ourselves again,' Alex murmured, her finger tracing the strong line of his jaw and settling on his lips.

He kissed her finger gently and then her lips.

The spicy odour of his aftershave lotion titillated her nostrils and she sighed rapturously. 'Justin, couldn't we move in here?' she asked. 'I mean, during the week. We could still visit your parents quite often.'

'Alex, it's not that I want us to stay with my parents, but at the moment, you know I'm away a lot and you'd be here alone.' Justin's lips teased her earlobes.

'I wouldn't mind that. I just want to be alone with you. I want to cook for you, for there to be just us when you come home. Oh, Justin, I want to be your wife, not a—well, not just someone who sits around waiting, trying to fit in with your mother.' Alex's voice caught on a sob. 'She . . . she doesn't think I'm good enough for you.'

'That's nonsense. Alex, you are my wife,' he said huskily, 'and that's the way I want it. Now, stop all this talking and kiss me like a dutiful little wife,' he chuckled, kissing her until she was breathless. His kisses deepened, his fingers twined in the silky softness of her hair, washing away all desire for talk.

The doorbell chimed loudly, gradually breaking into the intimacy of their embrace.

Alex raised her head. 'Someone's at the door,' she heard herself whisper.

Justin groaned. 'They'll go away,' he murmured against her lips, prepared to ignore the interruption.

'Justin, it might be important,' Alex pushed away from him.

'This,' he kissed her, 'is more important.'

'Justin!'

He sighed, 'All right,' and smoothed his hair as he went reluctantly to the door.

'Justin darling! How are you?'

The liquid voice drew Alex into the foyer in time to

see Justin's arms go round the other girl. Although the
kiss was brief it was hardly sisterly, and Alex stopped in
surprise. Over Justin's shoulder dark eyes sharpened on
Alex's figure hovering in the doorway.

The woman, for she was more Justin's age, leant back
and looked up at Justin. 'Have I arrived at an in-
opportune moment, darling?'

Justin turned around, his arms falling to his side.
'Would it make any difference if I said yes, Margot?'
He smiled at her. 'Come in and meet my wife. Alex, this
is Margot Donald, a colleague of mine.'

'Colleague? More of a friend, Justin, I hope,' she
admonished. 'So this is Alex. I must say you're somewhat of a cradle-snatcher, Justin. She's just a baby!'

'How do you do, Miss Donald. I'm older than I look,'
Alex said evenly, not liking the way Margot's scarlet-
tipped fingers rested possessively on the sleeve of Justin's
light sweater.

'Aren't we all?' Margot replied with a high laugh that
grated on Alex's nerves.

Perhaps Margot's laugh was the thing that Alex
disliked most about the other girl. Almost from the beginning she had felt that Margot was not the friend she
professed to be, but at that first meeting, still wrapped
in the security of Justin's lovemaking, Margot had not
really seemed a threat.

'Well, it was quite a surprise to hear that Justin was
married,' Margot continued. 'We were all quite sure he
was a confirmed bachelor.'

'I hadn't met Alex then,' Justin smiled easily. 'Would
you care for a drink, Margot?'

'Love one, darling.' Margot strode into the living-
room as though she was not a stranger to the apartment,
her eyes not missing the small dining table with the
candles still glowing, the soft music and dimmed lights.

'Well, I see I'm interrupting something. How cute and romantic!' She sank on to the couch, crossing her shapely legs. 'Come and sit down, Alex, and tell me all about yourself.' Margot patted the couch beside her. 'I can see you've changed the starkness of Justin's apartment already. Men are so hopeless when it comes to adding those little womanly touches, aren't they?'

Watching Justin pour the drinks, Alex subsided on to the couch, keeping space between herself and the other girl. The heavy perfume Margot wore seemed to settle cloyingly on Alex and she longed to get up and sit as far away from her as possible.

'I was going to redecorate the apartment for Justin myself some time ago, but,' she raised her hands expressively, 'I had to go to Europe with the company and—well, that was that.' Her smile slid from Alex's face to Justin's back as he fixed the drinks. 'Anyway, enough of that, tell me all.'

'There's not much to tell really,' Alex said, feeling uncomfortable and ill at ease, wondering just what Margot was implying. Was she trying to say that she had been involved with Justin before their marriage? Well, Justin was hardly an inexperienced youth. He must have been involved with other women, she knew that. Margot Donald was an attractive woman and Justin could very well have . . .

'Oh, come now, don't be modest, Alex.' Margot broke into her thoughts. 'Where did you two meet? It must have been a whirlwind romance.'

'We met in Brisbane,' Alex replied lamely, somehow not wanting to share any details with this sophisticated woman.

'Stop pestering Alex, Margot,' Justin remarked easily as he handed her a drink and then returned with Alex's orange juice. 'It must have been a case of love at first sight, because I knew I had to snap her up before she could change her mind,' he laughed, and sat down opposite them, his long legs stretched out in front of him.

Margot turned back to Alex, long false lashes hiding the expression in her eyes. 'And did you want to change your mind, dear?'

'No. No, I didn't.' Alex smiled across at Justin. 'I rather thought he might have changed his mind.'

Justin raised his glass to her. 'No way,' he said quietly.

'Ah, love! Where would we be without it?' Margot said theatrically. 'Justin's mother tells me you sing, Alex. In clubs, I believe.' Her eyes were cold as they looked back at Alex, her tone implying that it wouldn't surprise her in the least if Alex had added stripping to her accomplishments.

'I only sang as a hobby really at the Folk Centre in Brisbane. I was a student at the University of Queensland.' Alex told her.

'And what were you studying?'

'Sociology. I'd only just started my course.'

'I see. So now you've given it up to become a little homemaker,' Margot smiled. 'I hope you don't become bored.'

'No, I don't think I'll become bored at all,' Alex's eyes went over to meet Justin's and they exchanged a mutual look of unity.

'But Justin's work will take him away quite a lot,' interrupted Margot. 'Are you sure you won't be looking to find other—er—diversions?'

Justin's jaw tightened and his eyes, narrowing slightly, remained on Alex's face.

Alex laughed. 'No, Miss Donald. Justin's the only diversion I need.'

Taking a sip of his drink, Justin smiled crookedly

back at her, a cynical expression on his face.

'Such devotion, Justin!' Margot's laugh was high-pitched and harsh in the subdued light. 'Are you sure you deserve it? After all, you have been something of a rake in your time.'

'Reformed rake now, Margot,' replied Justin.

'For how long, I wonder?' Margot's lips pursed.

'How does forever sound?' Justin stood up and yawned, his light sweater pulling across the firm hardness of his chest. 'Well, Margot, I don't mean to be rude,' he glanced at his wristwatch, 'but we both have early rehearsals in the morning and I need my sleep.'

Alex flushed, embarrassed by Justin's blatant hint that Margot leave, and she couldn't meet the other girl's eyes.

'You're an uncivilised devil, Justin de Wilde.' Margot stood up. 'I really don't know why we women fall so consistently at your feet. Maybe we're all masochists at heart.' She walked across and touched her lips to Justin's cheek. 'I'll see you in the morning, then, darling.' She turned to Alex. 'My dear, I hope you haven't bitten off rather more than you can chew.' Her mouth smiled while her eyes were cold as they fell over Alex's figure.

Alex couldn't think of a thing with which to retaliate and she twisted her hands together. Sometimes the world in which Justin moved, the people he spent his days with, seemed so alien to her that a cold hand of fear clutched at her vulnerable heart. Was there not just a shred of truth in Margot's insinuations? How could someone as innocent, as unsophisticated as she was ever hope to keep the interest of Justin de Wilde, handsome, celebrated, sought after? Would he soon tire of her and look for someone else to please his jaded interest?

'She's a quiet little mouse, isn't she?' Margot directed at Justin as they moved to the door.

'Goodnight, Margot,' Justin said pointedly, holding the door open.

She pouted. 'Brute!' Her eyes went back to Alex. 'So nice meeting you, dear. Perhaps you can get Justin to bring you along to some of our little get-togethers, I'm sure you'd enjoy them.'

'Thank you,' Alex got out, thinking if all Justin's friends were like Margot she would be like a fish out of water.

Justin closed the door with a decisive click and turned to face Alex the expression in his eyes shielded by his dark lashes. He sighed heavily. 'Dear, divine Margot,' he said quietly. 'About as serene and sincere as a coiled snake.'

Alex watched his lips twist. 'Do you . . . do you know her well? I mean . . .' She stopped as he looked up at her, his eyes hard.

He gave a short laugh. 'We've known each other for some time. She's a top-rate performer.'

'Oh.' Alex stood watching him helplessly.

'Alex?' His voice was low, sending tremors down her backbone. 'Don't read anything into Margot's bitchiness.'

She kept her eyes on her hands. 'Do you think I've bitten off more than I can chew?' she asked quietly.

'Alex?'

She looked up then, her mouth dry.

'Come here,' he said softly, his voice wrapping about her, drawing her the few feet to stand in front of him. His finger traced the smoothness of her cheek, slid over the trembling contours of her mouth, down over her chin, down to the plunging neckline of her dress. Leaning slightly forward, his lips followed the trail of his finger, arousing Alex until she leant weakly against him, all thought of Margot wiped from her mind.

'What do you think?' he breathed huskily.

Tiny spirals of wanting began in the pit of Alex's stomach. They had always ended up in the bedroom, with Alex losing herself in the ecstasy of his lovemaking. That part of their relationship had always been perfect. They were two halves of one whole. It had always been that way. Any altercation they had was never carried over until the next day. No, the sun never set on any differences they had, until . . .

She rode the next wave into the shore and walked up the sand to where Paul lay stretched out where she had left him. There was no sign of Justin and she told herself she was relieved, refused to acknowledge the beginnings of a small niggling of disappointment. She dropped the board on the sand and shaking droplets of water from her hair on to Paul's sun-warmed chest had him sitting up indignantly.

'Ugh! Alex, that wasn't fair play. I'll get you back for that when you least expect it,' he warned.

Laughing, Alex dropped down on the sand beside him.

'Enjoy yourself?' Paul smiled indulgently.

'Mmm. It's so beautiful out there. Peaceful. Makes you feel that God's in his heaven and all's right with the world,' she replied.

'I was kind of suprised to see Justin de Wilde turn up at the beach with you this afternoon,' Paul said after a short silence. 'I saw him out there on the board with you.' He watched her closely. 'I would have thought he was a bit old for the surfboard scene.'

A spurt of irritation rose in Alex on Justin's behalf. He wasn't old, she wanted to say, but she remained silent, her eyes lowered, her fingers moving absently in the warm sand. 'We were just talking,' she said softly.

There was another silence.

'Look, Alex, I don't want to—er—well, to frighten you, but I think you should be careful with him.' Paul's hand rested lightly on her shoulder. 'He fancies you, for sure.'

Alex blushed. 'Don't be silly, Paul!'

'No, I mean it, Alex. He's got it bad. I should know— I've got the bug, too, and I know the symptoms.' He grinned crookedly and when Alex made no comment he continued. 'Not that I'm saying he's unsavoury or anything like that but, hell, Alex, he's miles too old for you, old enough to be your father!'

'Paul! Hardly that!'

'Well, just about,' said Paul, a little embarrassed. 'Anyway, what I mean is he's a man of the world, more experienced than you are. I'll bet he's forgotten more about—well, about sex,' he said quickly, 'than you've ever known. He's probably got a girl in every city he visits.'

A pain turned deep inside Alex and she raised wide eyes to Paul's worried face.

'Alex, I just don't want to see you get hurt,' Paul said intensely, drawing her against his shoulder.

She tensed for a moment and then relaxed against him and sighed. 'I'm not going to get hurt, Paul, so there's really no need for you to worry about me.'

'Oh, Alex!' He lifted her chin so that he could look down into her eyes. 'You don't know how ...' He sighed. 'You're like a babe in the woods when it comes to men. How did you manage to stay so ... so untouched?'

Alex could almost have laughed hysterically.

Untouched? If Paul only knew! She shook her head slowly. 'Paul, you really don't know anything about me.'

'I know you're a wonderful, sensitive girl,' he said thickly, and bent his lips to hers, kissing her lightly. When she didn't push him away he kissed her again, his lips cool and gentle, asking for a response.

Unconsciously Alex found herself making that same comparison. Justin was hard, unbending, demanding, lifting her to great erotic heights until she was sure she had entered another world on some higher plane. Paul was so very different, gentle, comforting, so much safer. So he might not touch her senses the way Justin did with just a simple look, wasn't that far more stable, so much less complicated?

Alex's lips moved on his, wanting desperately for it to be right between her and Paul. Her hand went to his shoulder as he gently pushed her back on to the sand. He was breathing quickly, his hands moving over the bareness of her midriff, his kisses hardening as he lost control and pressed his young body against hers.

Alex could almost imagine that they were Justin's hands moving over her body, Justin's lips on hers, and a wild surge of need rose inside her for a few seconds, before Paul's voice whispered her name and she came back to reality with a thud. An immediate coldness flooded her body. It wasn't Justin. No one could ever be Justin.

Tears rolled down her cheeks as she began to push Paul away with a panic that added strength to her struggles. But Paul was slow to recover from the shock of her sudden change of heart and his lips moved to capture hers again. Alex turned her head aside.

'No, Paul. Please don't!'

'Alex!' His voice was hoarse, angry. 'What the hell are you playing at? What is it that freezes you every time I begin to get close?' His eyes fell on the tears streaking her face and he sat away from her his expression a mixture of anger and despair. 'God, Alex, I'm sorry. I didn't mean to frighten you.'

Alex almost cringed with shameful guilt. Here was Paul apologising for something that was entirely her own selfish fault. She had led him on, encouraged his kisses. What else could she have expected? 'It's not your fault, Paul I . . .'

A shadow fell over the two of them and they both looked up guiltily, like two children caught with their fingers in the cookie jar. Their eyes met the coldness of light blue ice.

A pulse throbbed in Justin's jaw as he gazed down at their supine forms from his six foot of height, his eyes taking in the closeness of their bodies, Paul's hand still resting on Alex's bare waist, the tears Alex quickly dashed from her cheeks.

'Are you ready to go home, Alex?' he asked evenly.

Her eyes skimmed over him, almost apprehensively. He had pulled on his jeans and shirt and carried his sandals in his hand and from her low vantage point he looked incredibly tall and dominant.

'I . . . No. No, thanks. I'll stay a little longer. I can get a lift back with Paul.' Alex struggled to answer casually, although the words caught in her throat.

Justin's eyes were crystal barbs as they attacked first Alex and then Paul. 'As you like,' he said at last, and strode off along the beach without a backward glance.

'Whew!' Paul let out the breath he'd been holding. 'If looks could kill!' He frowned at Alex's pale face. 'Don't take it to heart, love. He'll just have to get the message that you're not interested.'

Alex watched Justin's fast retreating figure and shivered involuntarily. Somehow she didn't think it was going to be as easy as that.

CHAPTER EIGHT

On Monday Alex drove up to Brisbane to collect a few things from her flat, not returning to the coast until late at night, so that there would be no chance of having to see Justin. The following day she spent shopping, and if he did turn up at the flat she wouldn't have known as the boys were also away on a fishing trip.

Back at work at the restaurant on Tuesday night she went out on to the stage with a feeling of uneasy anticipation and her eyes skimmed the audience searching for a familiar dark head.

As the evening progressed she began to relax, and the night was almost half over when she saw him. He was sitting alone, at a table to one side of the stage, and he had obviously been there for some time as he had almost finished his meal.

Her eyes met his and he slowly raised his wine glass in her direction, a cynical smile touching his lips. Alex turned away, a dull flush suffusing her face, and she had to use all her willpower to keep from glancing back towards him.

In the first break Paul moved across until he was beside Alex and quietly remarked, 'Have you noticed who's seated off to your left, all alone?'

Alex nodded, waiting for her next song to begin.

'He's hanging in there, I'll give him that,' said Paul, and began to play the introduction.

By the time Alex was singing her final number she was as jittery as she had been the first time she had sung in public. With reluctance she went into the last chorus and she was incapable of preventing her eyes from turning towards his table. She almost lost her lyrics. The table was empty and although she searched the restaurant thoroughly she was unable to pick Justin out of the remaining diners and dancers. He had left without so much as a word.

The next day was the most hectic of Alex's life. The film crew swarmed all over the restaurant like busy ants. What seemed like hundreds of people flitted about with lights, light meters, cameras, make-up, clipboards, all seeming to know what they were doing. Alex saw Ben in a totally different role, that of a dedicated film-maker, and he was demanding of his staff and stars.

The morning went so well that they decided to shoot the remaining scenes in the afternoon, and it wasn't until the crew had wrapped up the equipment that Ben could finally have a quiet word with Alex. He informed her that she was invited to dinner at his unit on Sunday evening.

'I know that's your first night off, otherwise we'd have made it sooner.'

'Ben, I'm not sure it would be a good idea for me to come over,' Alex frowned. 'I mean, your parents may be upset if I turn up out of the blue.'

'Rubbish, Alex! Justin's already told them you're here, and it was Mum's idea that you come to dinner.'

Alex raised her eyebrows. 'Your mother suggested it?'

Ben grinned. 'Yes, honestly. You know, Mum's not so bad really. Her bark's worse than her bite.' He laughed at Alex's sceptical expression. 'Dad's as pleased as punch about seeing you again. He always said he'd have snapped you up if Justin hadn't beat him to it.'

'How is your father?'

'Fine. He gets tired easily, but apparently his doctor's pleased with his progress.'

Paul approached them and Ben gave him a calculating look. 'Well, I must be off. Pick you up about seven on Sunday.' He touched her arm and walked away.

Paul's eyes looked levelly at Alex and she groaned inwardly as he turned to watch Ben leave the restaurant.

'Ready to go back to the flat?' he asked clippedly.

Alex nodded.

'What did he want?' Paul jerked his head in the direction Ben had disappeared.

'Ben? Oh, nothing really,' she replied nervously. 'I . . . He just invited me to dinner on Sunday evening. With his parents,' she added guiltily.

'He invited you to dinner? His idea or his brother's?' Paul asked sharply.

'Actually, it was his mother's idea.' Alex began to get angry.

'His mother's? Why would she want to meet you? You hardly know them.'

'Paul, for heaven's sake, let's leave it,' Alex interrupted him before he could ask any more pointed questions. 'I'm tired and I want to go home, and I'm in no mood for an inquisition.'

They left in an uneasy silence that lasted the rest of the day.

In the peace and quiet of the study in Ben's unit Justin sat pouring over the papers his accountant had given him which he still hadn't had time to study. Hadn't had time? His lips twisted cynically. Hadn't had the inclination was nearer the point. Even now the typed sheets seemed to glare mockingly up at him.

He sat back and ran a hand over his face. Sitting here was a total waste of time, but he had had to use the excuse of this paperwork to satisfy his mother that he

wasn't sitting moping. He almost laughed. He was
hardly an adolescent, pining away for a lost love.

A spurt of anger coursed through him and he stood
up abruptly and began pacing about the small room.
Damn Alex! If only he could get her out of his mind,
out of his life. In six years he'd tried everything—
work, other women. Throwing himself into his work
succeeded in leaving him mentally and physically exhausted. Other women left him emotionally cold. Even
Margot. He sighed and sat down again. Especially
Margot.

He would have thought the night he'd spent with Alex
in her flat would have got her out of his system for
good. But it had had the reverse effect. Now he wanted
her with a depth of desire that surprised him, and the
thought of life without her nearly drove him insane. To
all outward appearances he was calm, refined, in command of himself, but inside he realised his control was
as easily snapped, that he could be as primitive, if you
like, as the next man. Where Alex was concerned, that
was.

Alex. She was the catalyst that set off the chemical
reaction and wiped away his façade of civility. But he
was determined to keep his cool from now on. He
almost smiled recalling the shock on her face when she
caught sight of him at the restaurant. He would make
sure she knew he was around and intended to stay
around.

Each night Justin sat at the same table at Christie's,
eating his meal, listening to the music, watching Alex
sing. He always left before the last song and made no
attempt to approach her, and Alex was totally perplexed
by his actions. As each evening passed she found her
eyes seeking him out as she sang. Most times he didn't

acknowledge her look, but occasionally he would raise his wine glass or smile, causing Alex's stomach to turn over with agitation. Paul took great exception to Justin's presence, and as the week wore on he began making snide sarcastic remarks about him both on and off the stage, and Alex's nerves stretched to breaking point.

Sunday evening arrived far too soon and Alex stood in her room trying to decide what to wear. She held up a sedate floral sundress and then returned it to the wardrobe. Tonight she needed a psychological boost to her ego so that she could face her mother-in-law with self-confidence and poise.

Her eyes rested on the new black dress she had bought a couple of weeks ago and hadn't as yet worn, and a smile lifted the corners of her mouth. It was just what she needed. She knew the dress suited her and if she wore it she couldn't possibly be reduced to the gauche little mouse Justin's mother had always made her feel in the past.

Slipping out of her bathrobe, she lifted the soft black material over her head and let it fall over her shoulders, its silkiness a caress against her skin. The bodice moulded her full breasts and accentuated her narrow waist, the shoestring straps exposing an expanse of tanned shoulders and back. The front was low enough to hint at the swell of the white skin of her breasts and her hair took on a fairer tone in contrast to the dark colour of the dress.

Knowing her days on the beach had added a healthy colour to her face, she used her make-up sparingly, only touching her lashes with mascara, her eyes almost violet-blue in her tortuous excitement. She slipped on her high heels and picked up a light cotton shawl for later in the evening when the sea breeze could become chilly after the heat of the day.

Her hair shimmered in the light as she gave herself a last inspection in the mirror. Taking a deep breath, she firmly told her reflection she was not going to be intimidated by any of the de Wildes. She was a responsible adult, a person in her own right, and she was determined to meet them on their own level. She glanced at the bedside clock. Ben should be here any minute now and she hoped she would have the courage of her convictions when she found herself in their midst.

Paul was sprawled almost insolently in a lounge chair in the living room and frowned up at her from his magazine. As his eyes moved over her his scowl deepened.

'I thought it was just an informal dinner,' he said curtly.

'It is as far as I know,' she said, refusing to be drawn.

'Humpf! Don't you think you've overdone it a bit in that get-up?'

Alex smoothed the dress nervously over her hips. Perhaps Paul was right; maybe she had gone a little overboard. Her eyes flickered uncertainly as she tried to decide whether or not to change her outfit before it was too late.

'Don't look like that, Alex.' Paul got to his feet.

'Like what?'

'All lost and ... Oh, hell, Alex, I'm sorry. I just don't think you should go tonight. Not looking as great as you do.' Paul came to stand aggressively in front of her.

'I said I'd go. They're expecting me.'

'Well, I don't trust those de Wildes as far as I can throw them. They could be bloody Bluebeards for all we know.'

'I hardly think so,' Alex smiled faintly. 'Not in front

of their parents, anyway.'

'It's not funny, Alex,' Paul growled with ill grace, and pulled her into his arms.

Alex put her hands against his chest and turned her head so that his lips touched her cheek. 'Please, Paul!'

He let her go and threw himself back into the lounge chair. 'I guess I come a pretty poor second to those two sophisticated, well-heeled, upper crust men of the world,' he said with self-pitying anger.

'Paul, you've got it all wrong . . .'

'Have I, Alex?' He looked up at her cynically.

'Yes, you have. But I can see in this mood it would be useless trying to put you right. If I said white was white at the moment you'd swear it was black.' Alex turned away and when the doorbell chimed loudly into the strained silence she was almost relieved to cross to open the door to Ben.

But it wasn't Ben standing in the hallway. Justin stood with one hand on the door jamb, the other on his hip, and looked so big and attractive it was quite a few seconds before Alex could catch her breath. He was wearing a light blue scrub denim suit, his slacks hugging his muscular thighs and flaring slightly from the knee while the short jacket moulded his broad shoulders and fitted into the narrowness of his waist. His dark blue body shirt was unbuttoned at the neck and was pulled open to show the darkness of fine hair on his chest and a gold zodiac sign glittering in the light shining through the doorway.

He smiled slowly, a little crookedly and Alex felt her knees turn to water. 'Hi!'

'Hello!' Alex said huskily. 'I . . . I was expecting Ben.' She turned back into the flat to collect her shawl and bag and Justin stepped inside.

Paul glanced up at Justin with barely disguised

antagonism, the fact that he was seated putting him at a decided disadvantage.

'Denman,' Justin nodded at the younger man, his eyes narrowed, slightly arrogant.

'I'll see you later, Paul.' Alex had to physically prevent herself from running to the door in case Paul provoked a scene.

Paul didn't even glance in her direction.

'Don't wait up for her.' Justin's hand took Alex's arm. 'She may be late,' he added loftily as he all but pushed Alex through the door, closing it decisively behind him.

'I take it your young watchdog isn't too thrilled about your night out,' he remarked as they stepped into the elevator.

Alex glanced across at him, finding him standing close behind her, closer than she expected him to be and her heart beat rapidly in her throat. 'I don't have to answer to Paul,' she said quietly, not wanting to cross swords with him before the evening began.

'He seems to think you do.' His eyes moved over her with slow deliberation.

'Well, I don't,' she snapped, feeling his eyes on her body as tangible as a touch.

'Then perhaps you should correct his misapprehension.' Justin motioned for her to precede him out of the lift.

'Paul is under no misapprehension where I'm concerned,' Alex said sharply. 'I'm a free agent.'

Justin didn't comment until they were both seated in his car and then he gave a harsh laugh. 'You know, you're a cool customer, Alex. If I didn't know better I'd say your veins ran pure ice.'

'I really don't know what you mean,' Alex sat stiffly in her seat. 'Can't we get going?'

Resting his arms on the steering wheel, Justin watched her with narrowed eyes. 'I mean young Denman. That touching and torrid little scene on the beach the other day didn't appear to be quite to your liking, and if you're as uninterested in him as you claim to be why give him the come-on? And why share your bed and board with him? It'd be kinder to put him out of his misery.'

'My bed and . . .' Alex stared at him incredulously, her anger rising. 'If it's any of your business, which it damn well isn't, I don't happen to share my bed with Paul or anyone. I'm so terribly sorry to disappoint you.'

Justin's expression barely altered.

Alex sighed. 'I seem to think we've been through all this before.'

'We've been through it before all right but you accidentally,' he emphasised the word, 'forgot to mention that the whole group was sharing the flat.' His eyes gleamed icily. 'Ben told me.'

'The flat has two bedrooms. Paul, Jeff and Danny share one room and I have the other,' she said flatly, turning away from him.

'Do you now?' he said softly.

'Why do I even bother?' she asked herself aloud as she put her hand on the door catch. 'If you want to misconstrue . . .'

His hand reached out and covered hers, preventing her from opening the door, his arm pinning her easily in her seat. 'Cool it, Alex,' he said softly. 'You have to make allowances for old-fashioned jealousy.' His breath fanned her cheek before she felt his lips on the line of her jaw.

She closed her eyes, wanting to abandon herself to the familiar ecstasy of his kisses, and knowing she mustn't allow herself to do it. But there was no need for her to have to repel him. He sat back in his seat and switched on the ignition, driving away without making any further comment.

As they drove the short distance to the unit Justin made light conversation and Alex could almost convince herself that she had imagined those few moments before they left the car park.

They completed the short elevator ride up to Ben's unit in silence, and Alex's mouth felt dry with nervousness. Her total recollection of Justin's mother was one of forceful disapproval. She had never been able to summon the courage to stand up to Grace de Wilde all those years ago. Even when she left Justin she had taken the coward's way out, had disappeared before his mother could use any of her intimidating influence on her to stay. That was almost funny. Any influencing Mrs de Wilde would have done would have been to separate her from Justin, of that she was certain. She was most probably overjoyed to see the back of Alex.

'Don't tell me you're nervous, Alex?' He half smiled teasingly. 'And here you'd almost convinced me you were now the ever self-possessed sophisticate!'

Taking a steadying breath, Alex refused to answer him, not letting herself be drawn, and he chuckled softly as the elevator door slid open. Alex hung back uncertainly until Justin took her arm and led her into the hallway. Standing in front of the apartment door Justin held the key in his hand, pausing before attempting to let them inside. 'Alex, before we go in there's something I'd like to say.' He glanced at her thoughtfully. 'My father's a sick man, even more ill than he's been told he is. Do you think we could bury the hatchet just for tonight?'

Alex looked steadily at him.

'One shock, an upset, anything, could bring on another attack and, as you will imagine, I don't want that. What do you say?'

She nodded. 'All right. But I never intended to do or say anything to upset anyone, Justin. Unless I was provoked,' she added quickly. 'You know I wouldn't knowingly hurt your father if I could help it.' A fleeting expression touched his face, an expression Alex couldn't fathom, and then he inserted the key in the door and the moment passed.

Soft music provided an unobtrusive background for the two men sitting chatting in the comfortable chairs in the living-room. Ben de Wilde was sipping a glass of white wine, but it was the older man who drew Alex's attention. To say she was shocked was an understatement. She could scarcely credit that someone could change so much in six years, that those years could age with such relentlessness a man who had been so vital.

Her memories of Justin's father were of a tall man, as tall as Justin with Justin's broad frame, his hair grey and his eyes twinkling blue. But as John de Wilde got slowly to his feet it took all of Alex's self-control not to allow her shock to show. He had lost a good couple of stone and his hair was completely white, while the skin on his face seemed to stretch across his cheekbones. She darted a quick imploring glance at Justin, but he had left her and had moved across to the bar to get her a drink.

Then her father-in-law was stepping forward to greet her and his eyes, perhaps a little duller blue than she remembered, were nevertheless full of the same laughter and her heart went out to him. His smile of welcome was as genuine as she knew it would be and she went into his open arms as though she had never been away.

'Alex, my dear! It's wonderful to see you again. We've missed you.' He hugged her and then stood back, his eyes moving over her face. 'Here, let me look at you. Still as beautiful as ever. More so, I think, don't you, Justin?' He turned to his elder son.

Justin had returned with their drinks and handed one to Alex. 'Most definitely, Dad,' he smiled, a challenging flicker lurking in the depths of his eyes as they met Alex's. 'I only hope she thinks I've worn as well,' he added.

John de Wilde looked enquiringly back at his daughter-in-law. 'What do you say, Alex?'

Alex pretended to weigh Justin up. 'Mm. Fairly well. He's still not as handsome as you are, though,' she grinned back at his father, and he laughed delightedly.

'Minx!' He sobered. 'It is good to have you back, Alex,' he said seriously. 'Justin's news was worth any number of the pills the powers that be insist on pumping into me.'

'Justin's news?' Alex frowned.

'Yes, darling.' Justin's arm came around her waist, his fingers exerting a warning pressure. 'I realise you wanted to keep it to ourselves for a while but I couldn't manage to keep it a secret from the family, especially knowing Dad would be tickled pink to learn we'd decided to get back together again.'

CHAPTER NINE

'NOTHING in the world could have made me happier, Alex.' Her father-in-law kissed her cheek as Alex stood immobile with shock. 'It means so much to Justin's mother and myself to see you both happy.'

Alex glanced from her father-in-law to Ben, who was looking carefully into his wine glass, before she turned slowly back to Justin. Her eyes changed from shock to cold restrained anger. Justin's lips touched her temple and he smiled down at her with studied tenderness, his fingers warning her again.

'Well, Alex, my dear. It's so nice to see you again. Quite a pleasant surprise.' Justin's mother had joined them, and she wasn't alone.

Her senses numb, Alex's eyes moved from her mother-in-law to the immaculately dressed woman beside her. There was a definite similarity between the two women. Both were tall, almost statuesque, poised, sophisticated, but while Justin's mother's smile seemed genuine enough, it was obvious that Margot Donald was not overly pleased to see Alex. Not that her smile of welcome wasn't sitting nicely on her face, but her eyes were cold as they slowly moved over Alex's figure.

No, Margot was not pleased to have Alex back on the scene. And who could blame her? Alex mused, almost objectively. Margot most probably believed she had Justin in her clutches at last, only to have Alex turn up again like a bad penny. Well, Margot could set her mind at rest. She could have him and she was welcome to him. Alex could almost feel sorry for her.

Mrs de Wilde crossed to kiss Alex coolly on the cheek. 'You look very nice, dear. So much more—well, grown up.'

The familiar feeling of inferiority rose inside Alex and she drew herself up to her full height. 'Six years makes a difference to everyone,' she said evenly.

Mrs de Wilde looked sharply at her daughter-in-law. 'Yes, quite.' She turned slightly. 'You remember Margot, don't you, Alex?'

'Yes,' Alex nodded. 'How are you, Margot?'

'Fine, thank you.'

'Margot was holidaying up north and kindly cut short her vacation when she learned we were staying here at the Gold Coast for a few weeks. Margot's schedule is so tight it was lucky she could spare the time to come down here.'

'I couldn't let the opportunity to see you both again pass by.' Margot squeezed Mrs de Wilde's arm and the older woman patted her hand.

'Your notices have all been good, Margot,' Ben spoke for the first time. 'I suppose you'll be off overseas again soon.'

'Perhaps.' Margot turned her eyes to Justin, soft intimacy in their depths. 'I've been trying for months to talk Justin into doing a tour of the States with me, but he's been quite reticent about it.'

An unexpected surge of jealousy took Alex totally by surprise and perversely she leaned closer to Justin's hard body, knowing that Margot's sharp eyes hadn't missed her slight movement.

'Justin must take a lot of credit for my notices,' she went on. 'Without a sympathetic and encouraging conductor—well . . .' Her hands fluttered expressively. 'And Justin gives me both sympathy and encouragement,' she said softly, her tone adding a hidden meaning to the words.

'You flatter me, Margot,' Justin replied easily, 'and underestimate your own talents. Your tours to Europe without me drew just as enthusiastic reviews.'

Margot pouted prettily.

'I believe you've been doing rather well for yourself too, Alex?' John de Wilde put in.

'Moderately well,' Alex smiled at him. 'We may not be setting the world on fire, but at least we have a consistent income.'

'Moderately well, hell!' broke in Ben. 'You're just fantastic, love.' He kissed the tips of his fingers to her and Alex noticed his mother frown at her younger son's language. 'Wait till you see my latest movie, Dad. Alex will be on her way to stardom, sure as I'm standing here.'

'Ben!' Alex blushed.

'No need to be modest, Alex. I mean it,' Ben assured her seriously. 'You have the face of an angel, the most photogenic face I've seen in ages. Of course, you may have to shed half a stone or so.'

Justin pulled her back against him. 'No way, brother. I like her the way she is. Pity Alex isn't interested in becoming a movie star,' he added firmly. 'She'll be far too busy starring as my wife.'

'Good idea, son.' His father's eyes twinkled.

'There's a lot to be said for chaining women to the kitchen table,' Justin teased, and at Alex's outraged expression his father laughed loudly.

'Something tells me you don't fancy that,' the older man patted her shoulder.

'Don't fancy it? Why, it's barbaric!' Alex spluttered.

'Not to mention a wicked waste,' added Ben.

Margot's laughter tinkled brittly, jarring Alex's already frayed nerves. 'Don't tell me you've become a male chauvinist after all this time, darling?' she asked

Justin. 'You'll frighten Alex off again, won't he, dear? No modern young lady needs to be reminded of the pre-suffragette era.'

'I can see this developing into a long and tedious argument,' said Grace de Wilde, glancing at her wrist-watch. 'I suggest we all sit down to dinner.'

The meal was not nearly as strained as Alex imagined it would be. She was seated between Ben and his father with Justin at the top of the table to her left, and Ben was his usual garrulous self, keeping the conversation flowing easily, even when Margot persistently tried to seclude Justin in their own private conversation.

The topics of conversation were general, Justin's mother saw to that, and no further mention was made of Alex's and Justin's reconciliation. But it was there at the very front of Alex's mind as she sat making a pretence of eating her meal, and she seethed with anger.

How could Justin have had the nerve to do it? How could he have used his father as an innocent accomplice in his sneaky little scheme? She wouldn't have believed he could stoop so low, act so underhandedly. If his father discovered the truth he would be both hurt and disappointed. But that was the point of it all, wasn't it? she asked herself wrathfully. Justin knew her too well, knew she wouldn't be able to deliberately upset his father when he was so obviously ill.

She cast a quick glance towards him and his eyes met hers, not flinching, with innocence, and Alex's lips thinned. He was a cool, single-minded devil. How she'd love to denounce him here and now, but of course she could never do it. As she watched him Margot's fingers settled on his arm, demanding his attention, eyes appealing, red lips moistly sensual, and Alex looked away in disgust.

'Grace and I will have to come along to hear you sing, Alex.' John de Wilde distracted her. 'I shall have Justin book us a table for dinner one evening.'

'John, I don't think you should . . .' began his wife.

'Oh, nonsense, my dear.' He smiled at his wife. 'You fuss too much. I have to eat, so what's the difference between eating here and eating at a restaurant? Which would be the best night, Alex?'

'Oh, any night,' Alex looked embarrassedly at her mother-in-law, not knowing which side to take.

'Well, I'll leave it up to you and Justin,' he said firmly.

Eventually they left the table and moved into the living-room to sit in the large comfortable chairs. Alex tried to appear relaxed, but she was waiting for the moment to tackle Justin, for the moment he was apart from everyone else. Anger bubbled within her and she could scarcely contain herself until she could have it out with him. With Margot monopolising him she was beginning to think she'd have to wait for ever, but she looked up to see him moving across the room while his mother was speaking to Margot.

Alex strolled after him to stand beside him as he gazed through the plate glass windows at the blanket of darkness bisected by the line of lights of the main highway and the moving headlights of the cars. Her anger, which she had been tightly curbing, threatened to burst from her and she had to prevent a tirade of angry words from spilling from her lips.

'How could you?' she got out quietly.

'How could I what?' he asked with casual innocence.

'Don't pretend you don't know what I'm talking about. You know very well.' Her eyes raked him. 'How could you do that to your father? How do you think he'll react when you tell him the truth?'

'Does he need to be told?'

Alex drew a deep breath.

'Leave it, Alex. We'll talk about it later,' he said curtly, turning as Ben joined them.

'What are you two lovebirds cooking up over here?'

'None of your business, mate,' Justin smiled at his brother. 'We were admiring the view.'

'Mmm. A likely story! Look, I was thinking,' Ben said seriously, 'supposing I swap rooms with you, Justin? I can take the study and you can have my double bedroom, so Alex can move in here.'

Alex couldn't hide the look of horror on her face and Ben frowned enquiringly from one to the other.

'We haven't discussed it yet, Ben,' Justin's own face held no expression. 'I may move into Alex's flat. But thanks all the same,' he added easily as Alex turned shocked eyes on him.

'You can't move in with me,' she got out at last. 'It's not my flat to begin with and—well, it's just big enough for the four of us. So I can't somehow see the boys being overjoyed about an extra person taking up residence.'

'For sure there's one of them won't be overjoyed,' remarked Ben drily.

'We'll sort it out later,' said Justin, slipping his arm around her shoulder, tantalising her bare flesh. 'Maybe we should take the bridal suite at the Chevron and have a second honeymoon,' he laughed, and Ben joined in, although his eyes watched Alex's pink face rather sharply.

'You don't seem very ecstatic about the new arrangement,' Ben remarked as Justin went across to the bar to mix himself another drink.

'There is no new arrangement, Ben,' she said, taking a shaky sip of her own drink. 'Justin's concocted the whole thing. He knew I wouldn't be able to deny it, not in front of your father.'

'Did he now?' Ben's eyes turned to his brother. 'Who'd have thought he'd be so ruthless? He *must* have it bad,' he grinned, and patted Alex's shoulder good-naturedly when he saw the angry set of her lips. 'It'll all work out, you'll see, love.'

'Oh, Ben, I wish . . .' Alex shook her head, feeling tears of reaction fill her eyes. 'Do you think your parents would mind if I went home now? I don't think I can face much more tonight.'

'Of course they won't mind. I'll tell Justin you're ready to go.' Ben went to walk across to the bar where Margot was talking to his brother.

'No.' Alex's hand went to his arm. 'No. I'd prefer it if you could take me, Ben. Would you? Please.'

'Hell, Alex, as much as I'd love to, it wouldn't be any use. Can you honestly see Justin letting me? No way, love. I'll be left to escort the divine Margot back to her hotel, something she'll dislike as much as I will. That woman reminds me quite vividly of a coiled snake!'

'Then they make a lovely pair,' Alex bit out, and then felt cheap and petty.

Ben frowned. 'Hey, Alex, don't let yourself get so bitter. Not over someone like Margot. Justin's not in-terested in her. If he had been he would have done something about it years ago, so any implications Margot makes about Justin and herself are all in her mind.'

'I don't really care,' shrugged Alex, her eyes on her hand as she absently rubbed her bare arm.

'You know, if you're going to be an actress you'll have to do better than that,' Ben chuckled.

'Alex, my dear.' Grace de Wilde's voice broke in on them. 'Come and sit over here.' She patted the lounge

chair beside her. 'We haven't had a chance to chat.
Justin tells me your parents are now living in Canada.'

It was some time before Alex could again bring up
the subject of calling it a night, and with an apologetic
look Ben moved over to the bar so that there would
be no disputes about who would be taking Alex
home.

'Perhaps you could drop me off after you've taken
Alex home, darling?' Margot smiled easily at Justin. 'It
would save poor Ben a trip down to Broadbeach and I
believe you'll be going that way with Alex.'

Poor Ben grimaced at Alex behind Margot's back.

'Sure, Margot. Are you ready to go?' Justin felt in his
pocket for his car keys.

'Of course. Whenever you are.' Margot bade Justin's
parents an effusive farewell, promising to call to see
them again within the next few days.

'Don't leave it too long before we see you again, will
you, Alex?' John de Wilde said as they moved to the
door. 'But we'll be seeing you when we dine at your
restaurant some time soon.'

The silence in the elevator was as loud as a clanging
bell to Alex's ears. Justin stood impassively between the
two of them, the sleeve of his denim jacket feeling warm
against her bare arm. When they reached the car Alex
almost ran for the back seat, leaving Margot to slide
into the front beside Justin. That this arrangement met
with Margot's approval was obvious by the flow of
bright conversation she kept up specifically with Justin
as they headed towards Surfers Paradise.

All the while Alex was aware of Justin's light eyes
watching her in the rear vision mirror and she determinedly forced herself to look away, staring unseeingly
out into the semi-darkness. They passed the street turn
to Alex's flat and she stiffened in her seat, her eyes lock-

ing with his in the mirror. His eyes narrowed before he looked back to the road.

Realising that she was to be dropped off first, Margot lapsed into a frowning silence and when Justin pulled up outside the entrance of the Broadbeach International she only mouthed a brief farewell in Alex's direction before climbing from the car. Whatever she said to Justin was spoken low enough so as not to reach Alex and her hand fluttered to his arm before she moved inside.

Justin turned and opened the back door. 'You may as well get into the front,' he said, leaning over to look at her. When Alex didn't move his jaw set tightly. 'Get into the front, or I'll lift you bodily into it.' His hand grasped her wrist and propelled her none too gently from the back of the car.

'Take your hands off me, Justin!' Alex flashed at him, trying without much success to free her arm. 'I'm afraid I don't go in for all this tough he-man stuff. It doesn't impress me in the least. I've told you before.'

'Impressing you was the last thing I had in mind,' he replied just as curtly as he closed her door with a restrained slam.

The air in the confines of the car fairly crackled with tension as they headed back towards Surfers Paradise. Alex gazed blindly out of her window, her lips set in a firm line. Neither of them broke the heavy silence until Justin drew up in front of the block of flats where Alex was living.

'Thank you for driving me home,' Alex turned to him and said with barely concealed ill-grace. 'And as to that other little scheme of yours, I'll leave you to tell your parents the truth whichever way you care to tell them, as long as you do put them in the picture.'

Without a word Justin climbed out of the car and

opened her door for her, preparing to follow her into the building.

'I can find my own way,' Alex's eyes met his defiantly. 'Goodbye, Justin.'

He smiled cynically. 'So final, Alex?' One dark eyebrow rose. 'Do allow me to see you safely inside. Your angry young man would want me to do that, I'm sure,' he added sarcastically, and his hand in the small of her back set her walking towards the floodlit doorway.

They rode the elevator in silence and it was with relief that Alex inserted her key in the lock and swung open the door of her flat. 'Goodbye,' she said rigidly, her hand on the door barring any entry into the flat beyond.

'I'd appreciate a moment of your valuable time, Alex,' Justin said evenly. 'I think we need to talk. About us and about my father.'

Her whole body tensed as she firmly blocked the doorway. 'As far as I'm concerned we've said all there is to say about it. Or, at least, I have.'

'Well, I haven't!' He in turn stood his ground, his tall, muscular frame seeming to fill the hallway. 'At least hear me out, Alex.' He rested his hands on his hips. 'Surely you're adult enough to discuss it?'

'Adult enough? Are you sure you're adult enough to talk it over without pressuring me?'

'No pressure, Alex.' He turned his palms upwards. 'Just simple discussion.'

A frown hovered on Alex's brow. Even as she stood aside she had a sinking feeling that it was a mistake to let him past the doorway, but she pushed her doubts to the back of her mind. Besides, with Paul here what could he do? Reluctantly she moved inside and he followed her, his face impassive.

The flat was completely quiet, although the living-room light had been left burning. The doors to both bedrooms stood open making it obvious that they had the flat to themselves. Paul must have changed his mind about joining the others at the disco. Alex could feel the pulse at the base of her throat begin to flutter as her body tensed in self-protection, building its own fragile barrier against the knowledge that they were alone together.

She threw her shawl and bag on to the couch and rounded on him, her chin rising determinedly, giving her a shell of self-possession, disguising her tremulousness. 'Let's not make an issue of this. I simply feel you were rather underhanded and dishonest about the whole thing. You knew I wouldn't go along with it, so why create such an impossible situation?'

Justin moved about the room and stood with his back to her as he gazed through the uncurtained window. His denim jacket pulled across the broad width of his shoulders as he sighed rather heavily and his hand reached up to slowly rub the back of his neck.

'I suppose I do owe you an apology, Alex,' he said at last, as he turned back to face her, 'but I'd like you to try to see it my way.'

Alex stood waiting as he paused, as though he was carefully selecting the right words.

'It's only been a couple of weeks since I saw my parents and I could see the difference in Dad in that short time. His condition seemed to have deteriorated markedly. When I mentioned that I'd seen you, it really brightened him up. You know how bad he felt about our separation.'

He prowled around the room again. 'I can't even recall consciously considering the whys and the wherefores or how you'd react.' He turned to face her again. 'It was totally spontaneous, not premeditated, believe me. What I actually said was that we were thinking over a reconciliation and I guess Dad took it as done. He was so pleased I hadn't the heart to set him straight.'

'What do you intend doing about it?' Alex asked quietly after a moment.

Justin shrugged. 'It's up to you.'

'That's hardly fair, is it?' Alex's temper flared. 'You're the one who started it, fabricated the tale, and now you want me to put it right.'

'You're the only one who can put it right,' he replied ambiguously, his eyes looking intently into hers.

She felt the heat of her rising colour and frowned in irritation. 'Must we go into all that again? You know how I feel about it.'

'I know how you say you feel about it,' he said with maddening calmness, 'but I also know that you're not being honest with yourself.'

Alex exclaimed angrily and turned away from him, folding her arms about herself. 'Don't start that again!'

'You aren't being honest, Alex, and you know it.' His voice barely held any expression.

'Oh, I know it all right,' she retorted. 'Of course it couldn't possibly be you who's deluding yourself, could it?'

He gave a harsh laugh. 'No. I'm under no illusions about you, Alex. Unfortunately you still have the power to tear me to shreds.' Alex's eyes flew involuntarily to his face as she turned slightly back to him and he smiled crookedly. 'And, you know, I'm beginning to suspect that you get some kind of sadistic kick out of doing it to me.'

Alex's nerves stretched as she tensed to immobility.

'Well, Alex, do you?' His voice was lower, rasping huskily in his throat. 'Have you developed sadistic tendencies over the years?'

'Don't be silly,' she got out breathily, turning away

again. 'You're just trying to twist the conversation.'

'Oh? And to what specifically am I trying to twist the conversation?' Although his voice was quieter she could feel that he had moved closer to her.

Powerless to move, she felt her heart thud loudly inside her as her breath caught in her chest. When his hands settled inevitably on her folded arms she stood without making any effort to repel him.

He pulled her gently back against his hard body, his breath fanning her hair, tantalising her senses. 'Oh, Alex, Alex! What are you doing to me? To us?' he moaned, his lips finding the curve of her throat, savouring its satin smoothness.

That same familiar fire raced through Alex's body and she made no attempt to escape his caressing hands, the arousing hardness of his body, the sweet stimulation of his lips. She began to tremble and with a catch of his breath Justin spun her around and claimed her lips in desperate abandon, reaching deep within her and finding an immediate matching response.

'Alex, if you're not going to go through with this to the end you'd better stop me now or I won't answer for the consequences,' he murmured as he raised his head to look down at her, his lips curving sensually, his hands moving caressingly over the smoothness of her bare brown shoulders, down to the swell of her hips to draw her impossibly closer to the solidness of his thighs.

His lips returned to touch her eyelids, her nose, to tingle against her swollen lips, his teeth nibbling her lower lip. 'Well, Alex?' he breathed urgently.

'We shouldn't,' Alex got out hoarsely. 'I . . . it . . . it wouldn't be right. I never meant this to happen again,' she stammered almost incoherently.

'Do you want me to stop kissing you like this?' he asked softly, his lips tormenting hers. 'Do you want me to stop caressing you like this?' His hands moved over her, intimately sensual.

Her senses had passed control and weakly Alex shook her head, her hands trying to unbutton his shirt, her body needing the closeness, the culmination of their lovemaking.

'Say it, Alex,' Justin whispered against her lips. 'God, tell me you want me like I'm wanting you.'

'Justin.' His name came with a sob. 'I . . .'

The door of the flat swung open and Jeff was the first to step into the room. When he saw Alex in Justin's arms he stopped dead, causing Danny to run into his suddenly stationary back.

'What the heck . . .' Danny began, before he too noticed that the room was not empty.

Justin groaned softly and when Alex went to push him away from her he held her tightly to him.

'Seems like we've picked the worst possible time to make our entrance,' Danny laughed a little selfconsciously. 'Should we go out and come in a bit later?'

'What's going on?' Paul's voice came from the hallway. 'What are you two cluttering up the doorway for?' He pushed Danny forward and the slight frown on his face deepened to a scowl as, face reddening, he caught sight of Alex still standing close to Justin.

She struggled to stand away from him, but he continued to hold her firmly. 'Let me go, Justin,' she appealed softly.

'Not on your life,' he said easily.

'Justin, please!'

'Seems to me like the lady wants you to take your hands off her, de Wilde,' Paul growled, moving past the other two boys to stand facing Justin.

Justin's eyes pierced the younger man and his jaw momentarily tensed. Then he smiled with arrogant condescension. 'The lady knows not what she says. I think she's really quite happy where she is.'

'Justin, you're embarrassing me!' Alex wished the floor would open up and swallow her. She was drawn in two. Although Justin was right, that she did want to stay held close in his arms, she knew Paul's feelings were being hurt and she had no wish to do that to him, knowing how easily angered he was of late.

Justin looked down at her, his eyes unfathomable, and reluctantly released her.

'Well, I'm for bed,' Jeff remarked, over-jovial with his own embarrassment.

'Me, too.' Danny took his cue. ' 'Night, all.'

As the two young men left the room Justin looked pointedly at Paul, who seemed to plant himself more firmly on the floor, obviously intending to out-wait Justin.

'Would you like some coffee?' she asked nervously of them both.

'Not for me,' said Paul.

'No coffee, thanks.' Justin put a sensual emphasis on the word 'coffee' and Alex flushed at his implication.

'I guess you'd better call it a night, then, de Wilde,' Paul said ill-manneredly. 'Alex has to work tomorrow.'

'Well, Alex?' Justin turned to her. 'Shall we call it a night?' His eyes met hers levelly, the demand in them throwing her into confusion.

'I . . . yes, I suppose so.' Alex moved jerkily towards the door. 'Thank your parents for me, for the dinner. I . . . I enjoyed it. And thanks for seeing me home.'

He looked at her with a mixture of angry exasperation and irritated annoyance, but she could see the fire of his passion still lying close to the surface and knew with a tingle of anticipation how easily she could send it raging to consume them both, how very much she wanted to do just that.

'Goodnight, Mr de Wilde.' Paul's voice cut rudely between them, breaking the bond that had begun to stretch across the room joining them together.

Alex saw the whiteness of anger in Justin's face and she took a step forward at the same time as he did. Justin's hand was reaching out to clasp Paul's shirt when Alex thrust herself between them. 'Justin, don't!' she cried. 'Don't hit him!'

'Hit him?' he sneered. 'Alex, I've had this.' His eyes turned coldly on her. 'We'll stay here or you're coming with me—make up your mind.'

'I can't,' she whispered.

'Alex, what's this all about?' Paul barked. 'You don't have to take anything from him. What's he got over you anyway? I'll call Jeff and Danny and we'll throw him out.'

Justin gave a short laugh and Alex put a restraining hand on his arm, feeling his tensed muscles beneath the sleeve of his jacket. 'There's no need for that, Paul. Justin was just going.' Her eyes begged him not to make the situation any worse.

After a tension-filled few seconds Justin shook off her hand and strode to the door, stopping when he reached it and turning slowly back to face them. His lip curled cynically. 'What makes me think you're half worth all this trouble, Alex?' he asked flatly before his eyes moved to Paul. 'Although you don't know it, mate, I'm doing you a favour taking her off your hands,' he smiled humourlessly. 'I think the time has come for you to put your friends in the picture, Alex, before I do. And believe me, if you leave it to me, I'll do it none too gently.'

CHAPTER TEN

THE silence echoed about the flat after Justin had left and the only sound Alex could hear was the beat of her own heart. She fixed her gaze on the floor as she felt Paul's eyes on her flushed face. The bedroom door opened and Jeff and Danny came slowly back into the room.

'Gee, Alex, we're sorry,' said Jeff. 'We didn't mean to break anything up.'

Alex made an irritated gesture with her hands. 'There wasn't anything to break up,' she said, guiltily knowing she had just told a huge lie. 'I . . . I think I'll go to bed.'

'Wait, Alex.' Paul took hold of her arm. 'What was he talking about?'

'What do you mean?' Alex couldn't meet his eyes, knowing full well what he was asking.

'Come on, Alex,' Paul's voice rose sharply. 'Don't play dumb. What did de Wilde mean by putting us in the picture?'

'I . . . I really don't know.'

'I think you do, Alex.' Paul looked down at her, his face cold. 'And I want to know what it's all about. I always thought there was something fishy about him, all smooth talking and looking down his arrogant nose.' When Alex didn't answer he shook her arm. 'Come clean, Alex. Don't you think I have a right to know?' he cried, angrily raising his voice.

'Hey! Cool it, mate!' Danny stepped forward and firmly took Paul's hand off Alex's arm. 'It's Alex's business as far as I can see. She doesn't have to tell us anything she doesn't want us to know.'

'That's right, Paul,' agreed Jeff.

'But he's got some hold over her,' Paul growled.

Danny and Jeff looked at Alex, waiting for her to deny Paul's statement.

She shook her head slowly and sank into the nearest chair, rubbing a hand across her eyes. 'I suppose I should tell you,' she said softly.

'I knew it!' Paul balled one hand into a fist and struck it into his open hand. 'I knew it! I didn't trust him from the first,' he exaggerated. 'I could tell by the way he looked at you, Alex. He was all but breathing heavily.'

'Paul!' Alex's face paled.

'Yes, give her a go,' Jeff frowned at his friend.

'We actually met seven years ago.' Alex's fingers laced themselves nervously in her lap.

'Seven years? You've known him that long?' Paul asked incredulously. 'But when you met him up in Brisbane a few weeks ago you never let on you'd met him before.'

'I know. I . . . It was a shock to see him.'

'But you must have been just a kid!' Paul's eyes accused her.

'I was seventeen.' Alex felt her throat go dry. 'We met and we . . .' she swallowed, 'we fell in love and we . . . we were married.'

'Married!' three voices chorused.

Paul's face paled and then flushed red as the other two glanced from one to the other.

'You're having us on, aren't you, Alex?' Paul asked at last. 'You couldn't be married to him. He's too old for you. He's bloody ancient!'

'You've said that before, Paul,' Alex said quietly, 'and he's not old at all.' She shook her head, dismissing the subject. 'Not that it matters. We've been separated for six years.'

This time the three young men passed no comment and Alex looked away from them. 'Until he approached us at Christie's in town I hadn't heard from him in six years. We hadn't spoken to each other in all that time.'

They sat in heavy silence, lost in their own thoughts.

'Are you getting a divorce?' Paul asked at last, and when Alex didn't answer immediately he stood up and walked around the room in angry strides.

'I'd like to talk to Alex alone.' He looked at Jeff and Danny. 'Do you guys mind?'

'No, I guess not.' Danny stood up. 'But stay cool. We'll go to bed.' He turned to Alex but made no comment on what she had told them. 'Well, goodnight.'

' 'Night,' mouthed Jeff, and they left the room.

As the door closed behind them Paul almost sprang across the room and leant angrily over Alex, his hands on either side of her clutching the arms of her chair. 'How could you do this to me, Alex? Why did you let me go on thinking there could be something between us? You could have been honest enough to tell me,' he bit out, keeping his voice low.

'Paul, that's not fair and you know it. I never lied to you about my feelings for you.' Alex met his gaze and at the hurt in their depths she felt her own anger rise as a pang of undeserved guilt fanned the flame. 'Now, let me stand up. I'm tired and I'm going to bed.'

'Not before we talk.'

'Your "talk" has all the symptoms of being an inquisition, and I won't have it, Paul.' Alex stood up, forcing him to move back, despising him all of a sudden because she knew Justin wouldn't have given in so easily.

'You could have told me,' he said with less vehemence.

'I didn't want to discuss it with anyone.' Alex went to walk to her room, but Paul put his hand out to stop her, his hold tentative.

'Why's he back, Alex?' he asked. 'I wouldn't have said you'd welcomed him with open arms.'

Alex sighed. 'I never wanted to see him again,' she said, and as quickly remembered how welcome she had made him the first night he drove her home.

'Does he want you back?'

She nodded. 'I'm ... I'm going to bed, Paul.' She walked to her room and opened the door.

'Alex?'

She paused and turned back to him.

'What are you going to do?'

Alex shook her head and closed the door behind her.

It was almost one a.m. when Justin walked quietly into Ben's unit. A light still burned in the living-room and as he stepped forward his mother looked up from a magazine through which she had been browsing.

'Mother? Isn't it rather late for you to be sitting up reading? Shouldn't you be in bed?'

His mother smiled wryly. 'That's supposed to be a mother's line to her son, not vice versa!'

Justin smiled faintly. 'Perhaps you're right. Well, don't stay up too late.' He went to walk past her to his room.

'I was hoping to talk to you,' his mother said quickly, and he paused, 'about Alex.' She could almost see his muscles tense.

'What's there to talk about?'

'I suspect that your reconciliation was something of a shock to her tonight.' She watched her son carefully.

'What makes you think that?' Justin sat on the arm of a lounge chair and folded his arms.

His mother shrugged. 'Alex has grown into quite a self-possessed young woman,' she changed her tack.

'She has that,' Justin remarked drily.

'When you were first married I worried about her youth. She seemed very little more than a blushing schoolgirl. And I don't suppose I gave her very much chance to be anything else. I've always felt just a little guilty about . . . I know I could have made things easier between us, but . . .' She paused. 'Well, no matter. That's all over and done with now.' She sighed. 'Margot seemed so much more suited to you.'

'Mother, I've never been in love with Margot,' Justin broke in impatiently, 'nor she with me. Margot's married to her career.' He felt a pang of guilt that these words might not be quite truthful, and frowned darkly. Margot would marry him, of that he was certain, but he was equally convinced that love had nothing to do with it.

'I realise that.'

His mother's words caused him to look at her in surprise and she smiled a little self-derisively.

'As I said before, the only thing I had against your marriage was Alex's age.' Grace de Wilde paused. 'Of course, that doesn't apply now, if it ever did,' she added graciously. 'Justin, I know how much you want this reconciliation with Alex, but if you're not careful, as Ben would say, you're going to blow it.'

If his mother had mouthed an obscenity Justin's face couldn't have mirrored more shock, and Grace de Wilde smiled.

'My head isn't completely buried in the sand.' She sobered. 'Alex won't be forced, Justin. You can't hope to pick up the strings as though nothing had happened.'

'Don't you think I know that, Mother?' Justin stood up and ran a hand through his hair, frowning impatiently. 'Look, just accept that Alex and I are back together.'

'Oh, I accept it, Justin. It would make me very happy. But does Alex accept it?' she asked quietly.

'She accepts it,' he added with an edge to his voice, and his mother sighed.

'Tell me, has she mentioned the baby?' she asked softly, feeling the flash of pain that crossed her son's face.

Justin shrugged. 'Not really,' he answered carefully. 'We haven't discussed it.'

'Then I think you should,' she suggested gently. 'You'll have to bring it out into the open or it will always remain between you.'

'Mother, I'm not sure I want to go through all this tonight. I . . . Look, just leave it. Alex and I will sort it out between us.'

'Well, I suppose you know best,' she said, her tone irritating her son even further, and at the stormy sharpness in his eyes she stood up. 'And I'm an interfering old busybody.' She patted his arm as she passed him. 'Goodnight, Justin.'

'Goodnight, Mother. And don't worry, we'll work it out.'

Justin stood in the living-room without moving, a hundred thoughts spinning around in his mind, wishing he felt half as confident as he sounded.

The de Wilde family booked a table for dinner at Christie's on Tuesday night and, as Alex had not heard from Justin, she would not have known they were coming if Chris Georgi hadn't mentioned the fact in conversation the afternoon before. The table was booked for seven-thirty, for five, so Alex surmised that Margot Donald was accompanying them.

As she applied her make-up she tried to keep her thoughts from tying Justin and Margot together. Surely Justin would have divorced her years ago if he'd wanted to marry the other girl.

A tap on her door interrupted her musing and her eyebrows rose in surprise when Margot herself stuck her head around the door before stepping into the dressing room.

'Alex dear, I hope I'm not intruding. May I come in?' Margot's eyes moved with barely concealed disdain about Alex's room.

Alex wondered what Margot would say if she refused her permission to stay and asked her to leave.

'What a nice little room,' Margot purred, abrading Alex's nerves.

Alex smiled politely. 'Thank you.'

'You appear to be doing very well for yourself these days. You were always such a shy little mouse. But then independence does give a woman dignity and bags of confidence, don't you think?'

'Yes, I suppose it does,' Alex replied cautiously.

'So nice not to have to depend on a man for everything, isn't it? Well, as one independent woman to another I'd like to have a little chat with you.' Margot sat on the edge of the only other chair in the room.

'Of course. What about, particularly?' As if I didn't know, thought Alex.

Margot laughed softly. 'Don't be obtuse, darling. Justin—who else?'

'What could there possibly be for you and me to discuss?' Alex asked flatly.

The other girl made a sweeping gesture with one hand and smiled mechanically. 'Quite a lot. As you know we—Justin and I, that is—have known each other for some considerable time. As students we were very,' she paused, 'close. But we both had careers to establish. Had I not gone overseas to study we would have married, but,' she shrugged, 'no matter. What does matter now is that we still have that—er—rapport, between us.'

Alex grimaced wryly to herself. Never before had there been so much left unsaid for her to read between the lines. 'I'm sure you have. Your careers run hand in hand,' she said carefully.

'I'm so glad you're intelligent enough to realise that, dear. It makes what I have to say so much easier.'

Alex's eyebrows rose again.

'I can understand why you weren't very pleased about Justin's little white lie to his father.'

Alex was unable to disguise the surprise in her face. Would Justin dare to discuss her, their relationship, with Margot? Margot, of all people? Surely not. But then . . . a small flicker of doubt lurked on the fringes of her mind.

Margot laughed brittly. 'Yes, of course I know about it. Justin told me his plan beforehand and I tried to dissuade him. But to no avail. Men can be so blind and so stubborn at times, can't they? I told Justin the whole thing was a little hard on you, but he assures me that as soon as his father's stronger he'll tell him the truth, so it won't be for too long.'

Alex fixed her eyes on the shiny surface of her dressing table, feeling all doubt fade away. Margot's and Justin's stories didn't quite correlate, and somehow she knew that Justin wasn't lying. She believed he had only told his father on the spur of the moment that they had been reconciled. That meant Margot was lying. Alex watched the other girl's eyes, not catching the merest flicker, and she clenched her hands in her lap. 'What exactly is the truth?' she asked calmly.

'Why, that you don't want to stay married. I know

Justin feels responsible for you, he's an honourable man. But I'm sure you don't want to stand in the way of his career, do you?'

'And how could I do that?' Alex began to seethe inwardly.

'He has the chance of a lifetime to tour with me. It will open doors for him professionally. Not that he hasn't done well already, but this tour will be the cream on the cake for him. But he feels you need him here, so I suspect he's going to let the chance pass him by.' Margot looked imploringly at Alex. 'You wouldn't want to hold him back, would you?'

'I never have before. Why should I start now?' Alex was controlling herself with difficulty.

Margot patted her arm and Alex had to stop herself from flinching away. 'I knew you'd be sensible, Alex. Justin and I are going to Brisbane tomorrow to discuss the contracts for the tour. It might be as well if you let him know, very subtly, of course,' she lowered her voice conspiratorially, 'that you think he should put his career first.'

'And do you think I'll be able to convince him?' Alex asked flatly.

'Of course. Why, you could use that handsome young man in your band, the one Ben tells me has a crush on you, to back up your story. I have every confidence in you, Alex.' Margot smiled again and Alex's fingers itched to slap her face.

'Well, I'll leave you to finish your preparations.' Margot stood up. 'I'm looking forward to your little show,' she said condescendingly as she left.

Alex sat where Margot had left her looking blindly at her mirror, her mind turning over with painful slowness. So Margot had now come out in the open. She had taken a gamble by stretching and bending the truth and in doing so she hoped to win Justin. Alex wiped a trembling hand over her eyes, her stomach churning weakly. Justin hadn't mentioned any American tour. But then they hadn't really talked . . . They never had in the past. Everything was running true to pattern again. Pain rose within her. And once again she could see herself being hurt, being picked up into the tide of Justin's life and being dumped on to the loneliness of the beach, to wait until he picked her up again.

She shook her head slowly. No, she couldn't go through all that again. Not for anybody. Not even Justin. And as she sat there, long after Margot had returned to the dining-room, Alex could almost feel the presence the other girl left behind in the cloying aroma of her perfume and the words that returned to taunt her.

'I knew you'd be sensible, Alex.'

Switching off the television set, Alex sat dispiritedly back in the lounge chair. The boys were away fishing and the quietness of the flat hemmed her in. Closing her eyes, she wished the past week into obscurity, out of her life, simply part of some crazy dream.

Had she really thrust Justin away for the last time? And if she had finally made him realise she didn't want a reconciliation on any terms then why was she feeling more wretched than she'd felt in her life? Tears rolled down her cheeks.

It was all Margot's fault. She shook her head. No— she had played right into Margot's hands. Looking at it objectively she knew Justin would not have discussed their marriage with Margot. And she knew there was nothing between them, never had been, no matter what Margot said. There was no one she could blame but herself. She was a thinking, reasoning adult, responsible for her actions. And in one evening her actions had alienated both Justin and Paul.

She squeezed her eyes tightly closed, but it was impossible to banish from her mind the scene at the restaurant the evening Margot had visited her in her dressing room. That scene would be with her for ever. What had made her do it?

Justin had approached the stage at the end of a dance bracket and seeing him coming she had turned to Paul. Deliberately she put her arm around his waist and asked him huskily to buy her a drink. Momentarily hope had flared in his eyes, only to die as he too caught sight of Justin approaching.

With eyes as cold as light blue ice Justin had stopped in front of the stage. 'May I speak to you for a moment, Alex?' he asked. 'Alone.'

'I'm sorry, Justin. Paul and I are going for a quick drink before we start up again,' she replied, steeling herself against his reaction.

Justin's eyes raked them both. 'It will only take a minute.'

'Can't you take no for an answer, de Wilde?' Paul growled, his brow dark.

Justin was unperturbed, dismissing the younger man with a look. 'Alex?'

'I don't think there's anything left to say.'

He looked at her for a moment longer. 'I think perhaps this time you're right,' he said coldly. 'Goodbye, Alex.' Turning on his heel, he walked away.

'Don't you ever do that to me again, Alex,' Paul said angrily. 'I won't let you use me like some spineless idiot. If you want a stone to throw at your husband you'll have to find another fool!'

He in turn had walked off and left her alone on the stage, and he had barely spoken to her since. Neither had she heard from Justin.

Her eyes filled and overflowed again, coursing down her flushed cheeks. At least Margot would be happy. It would be all plain sailing for her now. Alex dashed the tears from her eyes, trying not to allow the pain-filled memories to invade her mind. But they crowded in on her, and she was powerless to hold them at bay. For years she had kept the past out of her mind. She'd had to do it in the beginning or else lose her sanity. But now . . .

The numbness of the past years was wearing off, had begun to fade since the day she had accidentally noticed that small advertising brochure on the counter of the record bar. Justin's appearance had simply chipped away at the solid ice wall of defence she had surrounded that particular time of her life and only one small portion now remained locked inside her mind.

Perhaps she should surrender the rest, bring it into the open, make herself face it? And then maybe she would be able to come to terms with that too. If she really wanted to, that was . . .

Justin's face swam before her and her heart began to ache with her need of him. She had loved him then and she loved him now. When she had lost their child she had been distraught, so deeply depressed. So guilty. Guilty? She sat up, her hand tensing on the arm of the chair.

Why should she have thought she was guilty? Justin was the guilty party. He had never wanted their child. While she had wanted it desperately, hadn't she? Therefore there should be no guilt feelings on her part.

But she had known that Justin didn't want a family straight away. He'd told his family he had wanted to keep her to himself for a while. Yet when she'd been told by the doctor that she was pregnant she had been so sure that Justin would be as ecstatic as she was. It was all so many years ago now, she told herself, but the pain had not dulled one tiny bit.

She had dressed carefully that night, waiting for him to arrive home so that she could share her news with him. He usually arrived home by seven, but as the clock ticked over to eight o'clock Alex began to worry. He might have had an accident. Fear clutched at her and she stood swaying as she felt her heartbeats accelerate madly.

The telephone jangled at that moment and she almost threw herself across to answer it. At the sound of Justin's voice she sat down weakly as relief swept over her.

'Alex? Are you there?' he asked sharply.

'Yes. Yes, I'm here. I was just so glad to hear your voice. I . . . I thought you'd had an accident.' Alex closed her eyes.

'Of course I haven't had an accident.' He sounded short and Alex became aware of the sound of music, of voices in the background. 'Look, I'm going to be held up, Alex, so don't wait dinner for me.'

'Oh, all right. How long will you be?'

'I've no idea. I have to talk to the director about our next tour.'

'Justin darling, where's that drink you promised me?' The unmistakable voice of Margot Donald broke clearly into their conversation and then there was a muffled silence as though Justin's hand had closed over the mouthpiece.

'Alex?' his voice returned.

'Yes.' A cold little pain put a hurt edge on Alex's reply.

'Alex, I'll have to go now. I'll be home later.' He paused. 'Will you be all right?'

'Yes, Justin,' she replied flatly.

'Alex?' He swore softly. 'I'll be home in an hour or so.'

The phone went dead and Alex sat listening to the disconnected tone for a few seconds before she slowly replaced the receiver. Justin had told her there was nothing between himself and Margot. And yet she was always so possessive, so familiar with him. Justin wouldn't lie to her. Would he?

The background noise sounded as if there was a party going on. And Margot and Justin were there. Her eyes filled with tears and her breath caught on a sob. This was the first time he had ever been late. Was he tiring of her already? Was her youth beginning to irritate him? No, she almost screamed at herself. No, Justin loved her.

And when she told him about the baby he'd . . . What would he say? Fear washed over her again. Hadn't he always said he wanted her to himself for a while? Maybe he would be angry. No, he would be as happy as she was. Her hand went to the flatness of her stomach and her tears fell again. And if he wasn't happy about the baby what would she do? What could she do?

She stood up and set about eating her meal, forcing herself to swallow each mouthful, and then she moved about clearing everything away, keeping her mind blank. One hour passed and then another and still Justin hadn't returned.

Alex had never felt so wretched in her life. Her eyes were gritty and red-rimmed and she slowly undressed and donned her nightdress, looking in the mirror at the strained paleness of her face. So different from the happy face that had smiled back at her as she dressed, full of excitement.

How could Justin do this to her? Her anger rose as the pain began again. He had spoilt everything. Well, if he thought she was going to sit up waiting for him to come home then he was sadly mistaken. She marched across and slid beneath the sheets, lying tense and angry. But the loneliness of the large bed melted her anger and her tears fell to wet her pillow.

Of course sleep refused to come and her senses were tuned to fever pitch by the time she heard his key in the lock. The luminous hands of the bedside clock told her it was after midnight and Alex closed her eyes, feigning sleep, not wanting to talk to him.

She was acutely aware of his every movement as he went into the small kitchenette and poured himself a drink, then came softly towards the bedroom. He stood in the darkness for a moment before crossing to the bathroom, closing the door after him.

Alex swallowed nervously, wishing she could go to him cry her hurt out in his arms, but she stayed where she was trying to keep her breathing even as he re-entered the bedroom and began to undress. He slipped into bed beside her and she heard him sigh.

'Okay, Alex, you can stop pretending you're asleep and begin the inquisition,' he said flatly.

Alex couldn't trust herself to speak as a mixture of conflicting feelings rose to choke her—anger, hurt, uncertainty. Without a word she turned on her side, her back to him.

He bit off an angry expletive and his hard arm went around her, pulling her roughly over to face him. He flicked the reading light on over the bed and his angry eyes met hers. 'Alex, I'm not going to let you blow this up into a barrier between us. I'm sorry I was late, I just couldn't get away any sooner.'

'And Margot? Couldn't she get away either?' Alex asked quietly, her eyes on his firm chin.

'Margot was there, you know that, you heard her

when I was phoning, but I was not with Margot. That's once I've said it, Alex, and I'm not saying it again. I was tied up with Dan Martin.' He paused. 'Now, let's get some sleep, I'm dead tired.' He kissed her gently on the lips. 'Alex, come on, kiss me.'

Alex's arms went around him, and with a sob she buried her face in his shoulder. 'Oh, Justin, I love you so much. You aren't ... you aren't bored with me, are you?'

He laughed at that. 'Not on your life.' He moulded her to the hardness of his body, groaning softly as his hands ran over the contours of her, his lips finding hers, passion rising. 'Alex, Alex, how could I ever be bored with you?' His hands pulled her thin nightdress over her head. 'Mmm, that's better.'

'Justin, it's late,' Alex breathed. 'You said you were tired.'

The huskiness of his laugh had her own senses rising to meet his and he pulled her closer. 'I seem to have my second breath,' he said, and switched out the light.

Two weeks later Alex still hadn't told Justin about their baby. He was feverishly busy at rehearsals and they only seemed to have a short time together in the morning and late at night.

On Saturday it was Ben's birthday and they spent the weekend at Justin's parents' home. Ben was having a small party on Saturday night and lots of family and friends arrived. The house was full and Alex didn't see much of Justin as he circulated, talking to everyone, charming everyone. When Margot arrived Alex felt her heart sink. She slipped out on to the patio and stood gulping mouthfuls of fresh air, closing her eyes, resting her hot cheek against the coolness of the wrought iron patio rail. The closeness inside had made her dizzy.

'Hey, Alex?' Ben's voice came softly from behind her.
'What's the matter?'

She turned to face him, trying to smile. 'Nothing'
the matter, Ben. I just wanted some fresh air.'

He looked into her face, a frown on his handsom
face. 'Are you sure, love? You look pale.'

'I'm sure, Ben.' She sighed. 'Well, how does it feel t
be a year older?' she asked, infusing her voice with a
much bright normality as she could muster.

'No different,' he laughed. 'I think I'm going to b
another Peter Pan.'

'Then you'd better keep your eyes peeled for Wendys.
Alex laughed with him.

'I won't mind if they're anything like you, Alex,' h
said softly.

Alex's smile faded.

'Justin's a lucky man,' Ben said, and paused. 'I kno
how you two feel about each other, so why the dar
circles under your eyes, Alex?' He stood before her, hi
hands holding her arms lightly. 'And why the draw
look on that beautiful face?'

'Oh, Ben, you're imaging things!' Alex couldn't mee
his eyes.

'No, I'm not, Alex.' Ben persisted. 'And Justin doesn
look much better.'

A lump rose in Alex's throat and she put her fac
into Ben's shoulder and cried quietly. His arms held he
his hand stroking her hair, letting her cry it out. Sh
raised her head and looked at him, dashing the wetnes
from her cheeks.

'Feel better now?' he asked, passing her his handke
chief.

She nodded. 'I'm sorry, Ben. I don't want to spo
your birthday. I'm not usually so weepy.'

'Will it help to tell Uncle Ben all about it?' he aske

'There's not really anything to tell, Ben. I'm just a little depressed. Justin's been working so hard we haven't had much time together and I guess I'm just . . . just tired.'

Ben looked at her hard. 'I've got a feeling it's more than that, Alex, but I won't press you.'

'Ben, you're the best brother-in-law I could ever hope to have,' Alex tucked his handkerchief back in his pocket and stood on tiptoe to kiss his cheek.

'Well, well, Justin!' Margot's voice cut the air like a knife. 'Your brother's collecting a birthday kiss from Alex.'

Margot's tone belied the innocence of her words and Alex's eyes flew across to Justin. He gazed back at her, his expression unfathomable as he calmly lit a cigarette.

'You know me, Margot,' Ben said dryly. 'Any excuse to kiss a pretty girl, and Alex is much prettier than most girls.'

Alex felt herself flush. Ben's implication was not lost on Margot, and her mouth tightened. She laughed again and put her hand on Justin's arm.

'Perhaps you'd better look to your laurels, darling. Or someone might steal Alex from beneath your nose.'

Ben laughed at that. 'You can't steal someone who doesn't want to be stolen.' He strode across to the door. 'Come on, Margot, we haven't danced together tonight.' Before Margot could protest he had manoeuvred her in through the glass doors and danced her away, into the crowd.

Alex turned back to the rails, feeling numb and unable to face any repercussions Justin wanted to make. She felt him walk across to her and his hands turned her back to face him.

'Justin, please, don't say anything. I couldn't take it tonight,' she said tiredly.

'Alex, if I thought you and Ben . . .'

'Justin, don't!' His face swam before her and she clutched at him, feeling the darkness close in on her as she realised she was fainting for the first time in her life.

When she came to she was lying on the sofa in John de Wilde's study and Justin was bending over her, a frown of concern on his face. He had carried her in through the open glass doors from the patio.

'Alex?'

'I . . . I'm all right, Justin. I . . . I think I fainted.' She put her hand to her head.

Justin held a glass of water to her lips and held her head up while she drank some.

'I'm sorry. I've never fainted before.' She went to sit up.

'Stay there for a while, Alex. I'm going to get Bill Daniels.' Justin stood up.

'No, Justin. I'm all right now, I don't need a doctor. I was just . . . just tired and . . . and hot.' Alex hastened to assure him.

'I'm still getting Bill to have a look at you.' Justin said stubbornly. 'Now, just stay there.'

Oh, no. Alex wiped her hands over her eyes. Justin's uncle was a doctor and she'd have to tell him about the baby and he'd tell Justin. But this wasn't the way she'd planned to tell him. She'd just have to ask his uncle to keep it to himself. He'd understand.

When they returned Alex became so agitated as Justin hovered behind his uncle that the doctor asked him to wait outside. With Justin out of hearing Alex told him the truth and he made her promise to see her own doctor as soon as possible and to tell her husband. He gruffly reassured Justin that Alex was fine and Alex soon found herself tucked upstairs in bed, too exhausted and miserable to think straight. She slept fitfully, trying not to le her restlessness wake Justin and she dragged herself out of bed the next morning feeling so bad that she couldn't face herself in the mirror.

Her mother-in-law remarked on her paleness and Alex could barely stir herself to respond, and she knew that Justin was looking at her sharply.

'Are you still feeling ill, Alex?' he asked her, and she promptly burst into tears, rushing out of the room and up the stairs to their room closing the door thankfully behind her.

Of course, Justin followed her, pushing her forward as he opened the door. 'For heaven's sake, Alex, what's wrong? What brought all this on?'

Alex sank on to the bed, tears coursing down her cheeks.

'Alex, answer me.' His finger lifted her chin. 'What's the matter with you?'

'I want to go home,' she gulped, 'home to Brisbane.' She pushed his hand away and stood up. 'I don't belong here—I never have,' her voice rose.

'You're talking rubbish. You're my wife and you belong with me,' he said, his hands reaching out for her, but she evaded them, putting the bed between them.

'Please, Justin, I want to go up to Brisbane.'

He stood looking at her, his eyes narrowed. 'Alex, has this got anything to do with Ben? Because if it has I'll thrash the life out of him!' He came around to her his eyes burning with anger. 'Tell me, Alex, did Ben . . .?'

She put her hands over her ears. 'No, no, no! It's got nothing to do with Ben. It's me. I just want to get away for a while.'

'Alex, you're staying with me, and that's final,' he bit out quietly pulling her against him. 'Now calm down.'

'Oh, Justin, I can't!' Alex began to sob again.

'You'd better hop back into bed and I'll bring you a cup of tea. You look like you haven't slept for a week.' He smoothed the hair back from her damp cheeks. 'And tomorrow I'm taking you to the doctor for a check-up. I think you've allowed yourself to get run down.' He helped her undress and tucked her back into bed, and she was too dispirited to fight him. She looked up at him, a hundred worrying thoughts rushing about in her head.

'Alex, what's troubling you?' He sat down and held her hand.

Her eyes fell away from his. 'Nothing. I'm . . . tired. I think I need to sleep.'

He looked at her for a moment as though he'd press it, but changed his mind and stood up. 'All right. I'll bring you an aspirin.'

Surprisingly she was asleep before he returned and she slept until late in the afternoon. When she awoke Justin was moving about the room, dressing for dinner.

'Justin. What . . . What time is it?' She raised herself on one elbow, thinking how handsome he looked with his hair damp from the shower, his shirt unbuttoned and her heart contracted painfully, a lump rising in her throat.

It was funny how, after all these years, she could still remember how he looked at that moment, how desperately she loved him, how afraid she was of losing him.

'Almost dinner time. Do you feel up to coming down or will I bring you something up?' He smiled down at her.

'No, I'll get up. I feel better now.' Alex stood up. 'I'm sorry, I . . .' she stopped her eyes sliding away from him.

'Do you feel like talking about it?' he asked quietly.

'About . . . about what?'

'About what's upsetting you,' he said.

'I told you—I was just tired.' Alex said quickly. She couldn't bear to tell him here.

'Alex, come clean.' He strode across and turned her to face him. 'I spoke to Ben and he assures me that he has nothing to do with it.'

'I told you that, Justin!' Alex cried. 'You could at least have taken my word for it. Now I'm going to have a shower.'

'You're not going anywhere till we have this out, Alex. My God, you've been moping around for weeks, since the night I . . .' He ran a hand through his hair. 'Is that it, Alex? You're still angry about that night I was late home, the night I was discussing the tour with Dan Martin, are you? Because if you are . . .'

Alex shook her head. 'Let's leave it. I don't want to talk about it now. I just want to have a shower.'

'Well, I want to know what's going on?' Justin's hand grabbed her arm, his fingers bruising her flesh.

'There's nothing going on.' Alex's voice rose. 'And you're hurting me!'

'I'll hurt you even more if this goes on much longer!' Justin was almost shouting, oblivious of his family who could probably hear every word he was saying.

'Justin, stop it! Your parents will hear you,' Alex began.

'To hell with that!' he bit out, although he had lowered his voice a little. 'We're going to get this cleared up now. I don't intend it to go on any longer. For the last time, Alex, what gives?'

All the fight went out of Alex and she stood quietly. 'I'm pregnant,' she said at last.

'You're what?' he repeated in disbelief.

'I'm going to have a baby.' Alex watched his face carefully for his reaction.

Gradually he released his hold on her and stood back.

'Justin? I . . . you're not angry, are you?' Alex got out.

'Angry?' he repeated. 'I didn't think . . . It never crossed my mind,' he said almost to himself.

'Justin?'

He turned to look at her then. 'But we weren't going to start a family for a couple of years.'

'Don't you want the baby?' Alex forced the question out through lips stiff with shock.

'It's not that I want it or not. I just . . . Hell, Alex!'

'You don't want our child, do you?' Alex threw at him, her body aching with despair. 'Well, I do. And you can't stop me, Justin. I don't need you, I'll have it without you!' Her voice rose hysterically and she turned blindly, wrenching the door open, rushing headlong into the hall, scarcely aware of where she was going, only knowing she wanted to get away from him.

She knew he raced after her. She heard him call her name, but by then she was falling down the carpeted stairs, and she didn't recall anything more until she woke up in the sterile whiteness of her hospital room, blinking at the young nurse who smiled down at her.

'Good morning, Mrs de Wilde,' she said quietly. 'Your husband will be so pleased to see you awake.'

'No. No!' she cried, tossing about agitatedly. 'No, I don't want to see him. Don't let him in here!'

The doctor was called and she was given something to calm her down and the next time she awoke the doctor himself was looking down at her. 'How do you feel now, Mrs de Wilde?'

'Floating,' she said, and gladly accepted the glass of liquid the nurse held for her.

The doctor rubbed his hand over his jaw. 'Do you

remember waking up this morning?' he asked.

Alex frowned. She remembered something. It was all so hazy. She'd been upset about something. What was it? Her hand went to her stomach and her eyes flew to the doctor's face. 'My baby? Is it all right? Have I had my baby?' Her thoughts faded back and forth.

'Now, now, none of that.' The doctor took her hand, feeling for her pulse. 'We can't have you upsetting yourself again.'

A sensation of loss seeped into Alex's numb body and she closed her eyes. 'I've lost my baby, haven't I?' she asked flatly.

'Now, Mrs de Wilde . . .' the doctor began.

'I'm all right, doctor. But please tell me. I've lost my baby, haven't I?'

The doctor nodded. 'I'm afraid so. We couldn't save the child, but you've been a very lucky young woman. The fall down the steps didn't do as much damage as it could have done and you'll be able to have other children.'

Alex shook her head slowly, the whole thing coming back to her. Rushing away from Justin. All that went before her fall down the stairs. He hadn't wanted the baby, and now he didn't have to have it.

'Your husband is very anxious to see you, Mrs de Wilde,' the doctor said softly, and Alex turned her face into her pillow. 'Mrs de Wilde, he's been very worried about you. All your family have.'

'I don't want to see anyone,' she said flatly.

'Mrs de Wilde . . .'

'I don't want to see him,' she repeated, calmly, without expression.

There was a short silence. 'All right.' The doctor left and Alex lay with her face to the wall wishing fervently that she could have stayed in the oblivion of sedation.

Two days later Justin burst into her room with scant regard for the young nurse who tried to stop him. 'My wife is going to see me if I have to cross swords with the Medical Superintendent!' Alex heard him say, and then he was standing looking down at her.

'I don't want to talk to you, Justin,' she said flatly, amazing herself at the complete calmness that allowed her to sit back against the pillows and regard him without feeling.

'Well, I want to talk to you,' he said, obviously controlling himself with difficulty. 'Do you know how long I've waited out there for you to come to your senses? God, Alex, what are you trying to do to me?'

'I'm not trying to do anything, Justin. I simply don't want to talk to you, or see you, ever again.' It was incredible how easy it was to say it. It was as though all feeling for him had died. She could look at him without one spark of the attraction she once felt. There was no tingling in the pit of her stomach.

'Alex.' He sat down on the bed and pulled her into his arms. 'You don't mean that. You're not making sense. I love you.'

Her pulse beat normally. There was no catch in her breath at his handsomeness. There was nothing.

'Let me go, Justin. It's over. I don't want you any more, so please leave.'

He released her slowly and stood up, his eyes watching her. 'Alex, I'm sorry about the baby. What more can I say?' A flicker of pain passed over his features, but Alex was unmoved. 'If I could turn back the clock, I would, believe me.'

'I'm afraid it's too late for that. Quite simply, I can look at you now and feel absolutely nothing—no love, no hate. I'm indifferent.'

At that moment the young nurse returned with two

orderlies and Alex looked at them blandly. 'My husband was just leaving.'

For a moment Justin looked murderous and then he turned on his heel and strode out of the room.

'Are you all right, Mrs de Wilde?' asked the young nurse anxiously.

'I'm fine, nurse. In fact, I wonder if you'd tell Sister Green that I want to discharge myself as soon as possible.'

She flew to Brisbane next day, spending a couple of weeks with an aunt until she felt recovered enough to look for a flat and a job. She knew Justin came to her parents to find her, but Alex had made them swear not to tell him where she was, and they had done as she asked and for six years she had shut Justin out of her life.

CHAPTER ELEVEN

YES, the coldness of those years had gone now, had melted away, and there was no way she could delude herself into believing she was still indifferent to him. He had told her he wanted a reconciliation and if she had been honest with herself from the beginning she would have admitted that she wanted it too. And for some perverse reason she had pushed him away again and again, this time for probably the last time. He had never been interested in Margot and she doubted he ever would be. So why had she done it?

Alex stood up and paced across the room in despair, her arms wrapped about herself.

Had she wanted her pound of flesh, wanted to make him suffer the way she had? But in doing that she had only brought more pain on herself. Could it be too late to put things right between them? If she thought it would do any good she would ring Justin and tell him she had changed her mind, that she couldn't contemplate facing life without him again, that her life alone stretched before her like a barren desert.

She would ring him. What did she have to lose? The phone in Ben's unit rang hollowly and no one came to answer it. More dejected than ever, Alex slowly replaced the receiver. He must still be in Brisbane with Margot.

Her hand remained resting on the telephone when the pealing of the instrument almost frightened her out of her wits, so much so that she was unable to speak when she put the receiver to her ear.

'Alex? Is that you?'

'Justin?' Alex whispered breathlessly, not daring to believe the sound of his voice.

'Alex, I'm afraid I've got some bad news. I'm down at the Southport Hospital. Dad's had another attack.'

'Oh, no. How ... how bad is it?'

'We don't know yet. Bad enough, I guess.' His voice mirrored his concern. 'He's in intensive care. Ben and I are here with Mother.'

'Do you want me to come down?'

There was a brief silence. 'I think Mother would appreciate having you here, Alex,' he said softly.

'All right. The boys have borrowed my car, so I'll get a taxi. I should be there in twenty minutes.'

'Thanks, Alex. I'll see you then.'

The next few hours were harrowing and throughout those dragging hours Alex sat beside her mother-in-law who clasped Alex's hand tightly until Alex's fingers went dead. And she watched Grace de Wilde grow old before her eyes. Ben sat quietly while Justin paced intermittently, his brow furrowed, the lines on either side of his mouth etched deeply with fatigue and tension.

When a white-coated young doctor came into the room the four of them stepped forward together, like puppets pulled on the end of the same string. In those first few seconds Alex noticed subconsciously that the doctor had kindly eyes behind his horn-rimmed spectacles and then she realised he was smiling faintly.

'Mr de Wilde is resting comfortably now,' he said, and Grace broke down and wept on Alex's shoulder.

As she tried to soothe her mother-in-law Alex's eyes went to Justin and she saw his body sag with relief.

'Perhaps Mrs de Wilde would feel better if she peeped in on her husband,' continued the doctor. 'He's asleep, of course, but it will set her mind at rest.'

Later Ben drove his mother home and once more Alex

found herself seated beside Justin in his hire car. He drove slowly, his features tired and strained.

'You'd better come up for some coffee before you drive home,' Alex said softly as he parked the car in front of her block of flats.

He sighed tiredly. 'I think I'll take you up on that. In this state I'm likely to fall asleep at the wheel.'

Inside the flat he shed his jacket and tie and sat thankfully in a lounge chair, his head back, his eyes closed.

While she waited for the water to boil Alex quickly made him an omelette. It would have been hours since he'd eaten. As she set the tray on the coffee table in front of him his eyes opened reluctantly.

'Mmm! That smells divine.' He took a sip of his coffee and then attacked the omelette. 'I didn't have time to eat when I got back. I went straight to the hospital.'

'I thought you might have. Did . . . Did you have a successful trip?' Alex asked, although the words almost stuck in her throat.

Justin's eyes rested on her enquiringly.

'Margot told me you and she were going up to the city,' she explained. 'I believe you both may be off to the States.'

'Oh,' he said thoughtfully, 'I'm afraid I wasn't interested in the tour. Margot will be working with a top American conductor.' He returned to finishing his meal. 'That was great.' He replaced his empty plate on the tray at last and looked up at her.

Alex flushed, suddenly embarrassed by their closeness, the warmth in his eyes, and the silence stretched, tension-filled, between them. His eyes seemed to rove over her face returning always to the quiver of her lips and Alex clasped her dampened palms together in her lap.

'I'm glad your father has pulled through.' She broke

the silence at last, trying to bring the atmosphere back to normality. 'He's a wonderful man.'

He nodded. 'You two seem to have a mutual admiration society going. Dad forever sings your praises, too.' There was that same charged silence. 'I don't suppose there's an opening for another member of the society, is there? A life member?' His eyes moved over her and Alex stood up nervously, moving around so that he couldn't see her face. She heard the lounge chair creak as he too stood up, and it was no surprise when his arms moved gently around her. His chin rested on her shoulder, his breath tingling against her earlobe. Alex's heart beat a wild tattoo, but instead of turning her to his kiss he sighed softly.

'Alex, let me stay?' His voice asked quietly. 'No funny business, I promise. God knows I'm dead tired.'

'I've . . . my bed's only three-quarter size.' Alex's lips moved stiffly. 'But you can use one of the beds in the other room.'

'Damn the other beds,' he said. 'I need to hold you, Alex. You have my word that's all it will be.'

She turned around then and after one look at his face, almost grey with fatigue, she nodded, her heart filling with love for him.

As she settled in the well remembered circle of his arms Alex sighed. Perhaps tomorrow she would have her chance to apologise to him, to tell him just how much she loved him, had never stopped loving him.

The corners of Alex's mouth lifted blissfully and she murmured appreciatively, not wanting to open her eyes. She was floating in such a wonderful dream, held protectively against the warm firmness of Justin's body, feeling the tingle of his breath against her cheek. And then he was softly touching the tip of her nose with his lips. She could almost believe the magical sensations were real. Sighing, she fluttered her lashes open, only to meet the light blue of Justin's eyes, his face almost too close for her to focus clearly on him. Colour suffused her face and she swallowed convulsively.

'Thanks for last night, Alex,' he said seriously. 'For what you did for Mother,' he paused, 'and me.'

He made no move to hold her closer, although she badly wanted him to do just that. And she could feel the tension in him. Had she actually dreamed that earlier closeness, the feather-soft touch of his kiss?

'I'm just glad your father came through it,' she said. Some of his tension transmitted itself to her and her eyes were compelled back to his face. He looked so tired and drawn that her heart went out to him.

The colour actually rose in Justin's cheeks. 'Alex!' His voice came out huskily, tortured. 'Don't look at me like that. Please! I gave you my word last night. Don't make me break it.'

A dimple flashed in Alex's cheek. 'Oh, yes, I remember. No funny business, wasn't it?'

'Alex!' he said warningly.

'Funny business?' she teased, running a finger through the soft curling hair on his chest. 'That's hardly a very romantic description, darling,' she chuckled.

His hand moved to cover hers as it lay on his chest and their eyes met, flaring with their mutual wanting. Justin shook his head slowly. 'Alex, oh, Alex,' he said softly. 'Do you know what you're doing to me?'

'Something like what you're doing to me, I hope,' she whispered shyly.

His lips touched hers gently, tentatively, as though he suspected he was hallucinating and that any moment the beautiful bubble would burst. Alex moved closer, her body moulding itself along the contours of his and his arms bound her to him, his lips hardening, demanding a response Alex was oh, so willing to give.

'Alex, am I dreaming this?' he asked against her ear, sending shivers of delight through her awakening senses.

'I love you so much, Justin,' she whispered, 'so very much.'

He let his breath out slowly and Alex looked up at him with all reservations gone. He shook his head again in almost dazed disbelief. 'I couldn't begin to tell you how much I've wanted to hear you say that. At times I thought I was reaching for the impossible.'

'I'm sorry, Justin. I was so mixed up and hurt. I've been foolish,' she paused. 'There never has been anyone but you. Will you . . . will you forgive me?'

He put a finger against her lips, his eyes pain-filled. 'There's nothing to forgive. I'm the one who needs forgiving, who showed a total lack of understanding. I let you down when you needed me most. That's something I'll always have to answer for and learn to live with.'

'No.' Alex shook her head emphatically. 'It wasn't totally your fault. It was mine as well. I'd made up my mind before we even arrived in Sydney that your family weren't going to like me, so I didn't even try to fit in. If I hadn't been so absolutely wrapped up in my own rosy little world I could have formed a better relationship with your mother. I know I could have.'

'Don't upset yourself, love.' Justin ran his hand over her hair smoothing it back from her face. 'Let's put it behind us, start afresh.'

'No, Justin, I have to get it all off my chest. It's been bottled up inside me for years and I haven't been able to let it out. I have to try to explain to you how I feel, how I felt back then,' Alex said earnestly. 'I want everything to be right between us.'

'Everything *will* be right between us,' he said with conviction, showing some of his old arrogance. 'I don't intend anything to come between us again.' His finger moved gently down her cheek. 'Alex, that's a promise, one I'm going to do everything in my power to keep, believe me.'

Alex closed her eyes, putting her lips to his hand. 'Oh, Justin, it's been hell without you. I was just going through the motions of living—eating, sleeping, working. And as for—well, other men,' she looked up at him, 'I couldn't . . . when they touched me there was nothing. I'd buried that part of me away when I left you.'

A flicker of pain passed over his face. 'Alex? That afternoon, in the hospital, did you mean what you said? About not wanting me?' he asked quietly.

Alex nodded slowly. 'I did at the time. I was absolutely inconsolable about . . . about the baby. I wanted to hurt you as much as I was hurt. I didn't even attempt to see the situation from your side of it. I was so wrapped up in my own grief I didn't want to recognise yours.' Now that it was all coming out Alex felt as though a weight was beginning to lift from her. 'For a long time now I've been refusing to allow myself to admit that I acted badly, inexcusably. I forgot that the baby was part of you, too. Selfishly, all I felt was my own loss.'

'You had every right to forget my part in our baby, Alex,' he said quietly. 'Looking back, I can scarcely believe I could have treated you so badly. I'm not proud of myself. But at the time the whole crazy thing seemed to be getting out of my control—my work, our relationship. I couldn't seem to find a level where I could communicate with you the way we used to when we were first married. I could see you falling apart, but I couldn't seem to do a damn thing about it. I just acted like a spoilt juvenile.' He shook his head. 'I still can't put my finger on exactly what went wrong.'

'I think it was just a whole series of misconceptions on both our parts,' said Alex. 'Perhaps we were both guilty of not looking at ourselves realistically. I know I had you cast as no less than a knight in shining armour.'

He laughed self-derisively. 'And God knows, I was hardly that. When I met you you completely captivated me. You were such a refreshing change from the false showy world I moved in I guess I was terrified to let you mix in with them in case you wanted to grow away from me. I was jealous as hell of anyone or anything that might take even part of you away from me—Ben, the whole damn outside world. And God help me, even our child.'

'Oh, Justin, you've never had a thing to worry about on that score,' Alex told him sincerely.

'I think I know that now, but then . . .' He crushed her to him. 'As I said, I've got a lot to answer for.' He kissed her lingeringly and Alex snuggled into his arms, sighing happily.

'You know, at the hospital when you told me you never wanted to see me again I think I went a little mad,' he told her. 'Guilt ate away at me for weeks before I got up the courage to try to find you. And when I approached your parents they gave me the coldest shoulder you could imagine. It wasn't hard for me to believe you hated my guts. No one could have hated me more than I hated myself.'

'I didn't really hate you, Justin,' Alex's voice caught on a sob. 'Even when I was sending you away a part of me was crying out for you to stay.'

Justin sighed and shook his head. 'For two reasonably rational adults we've spent so much wasted time acting like children, haven't we?'

Alex dashed the tears from her eyes and nodded.

'I may not be a knight in shining armour, but as a very fallible man I love you more than I can tell you,' he said huskily, his arms wrapped around her, binding her to him.

'And I love you, too.' Alex's voice caught on a sob. 'We've got so much lost time to make up for.'

'Alex? About the baby.' His eyes held hers. 'We can have other children. Although I know I can't change the fact that no other child will bring back the one we lost.'

'Are you . . . are you sure you want a family, Justin? I mean, I can accept it if you don't. I just can't live without you.' Her eyes filled with tears again and Justin leant down and kissed her gently, tenderly.

'We'll have a round dozen, if you like,' he grinned shakily, then held her fiercely against him.

When she could breathe again Alex looked up at him teasingly. 'A round dozen?' she spluttered. 'Don't you think that might be setting yourself an insurmountable task?'

'Underestimating me, are you now?' he asked with mock sternness. 'I'll admit I'm a little rusty, but we can remedy that right now,' he said, and she went willingly into the rapturously demanding circle of his strong arms.

A GREAT CONDUCTOR

Those of you who were privileged to read any or all of Mary Burchell's *Warrender* books—published in a special 1978 set after being previously published as Romances—doubtless have a warm spot in your heart for the character of Oscar Warrender, the talented and attractive conductor. Few readers know, however, that Mary Burchell actually modeled this character on a real person: the tall distinguished, devastatingly handsome Austrian conductor and librettist of the first half of this century, Clemens Krauss.

Krauss was one of the leading conductors of his day, and his life was just as romantic as Oscar's. For like Oscar, Clemens Krauss fell in love with and married an opera singer—Viorica Ursuleac, a leading soprano of the twenties and thirties.

Clemens Krauss was born in Vienna in 1893. His musical ability showed early, and by 1922 he was already a renowned conductor performing at all the great opera houses and concert halls of Europe. In 1929 he was appointed director of the Vienna state opera, one of the most important positions a conductor could achieve. In 1934 he moved to Berlin where he directed that state opera; in 1936 he went to Munich to direct the opera there. As well as conducting, Krauss worked with the well-known composer Richard Strauss and wrote the libretto for Strauss's opera *Capriccio*.

After the Second World War Krauss went to South America, where he was guest conductor at a number of important concerts and operas. He was still as devoted to his wife, Viorica, as he had been in his youth—and still as devoted to music. He died in Mexico City in 1954 just after conducting a triumphant concert. Musicians and music lovers all over the world mourned the passing of a great and talented man.